They'd ba

And now she was stuck on a collection of ~~boul~~
no more than five feet in diameter, marooned over
the gushing waters of the Virgin River with a man
she didn't know. They'd been lucky. If she and Elias
had been even ten feet behind, they wouldn't have
survived the crush of the flood.

Agent Broyles. Using his first name humanized him.

Sayles swept her hair out of her face and came away
with a handful of rainwater as she took a seat. Closer
than she wanted to be to Agent Broyles, but there
was nowhere else to go and they were in for the long
haul as of right now. "Are you injured?"

"No." He shook his head, droplets flinging every
which way, and threaded his hands into his hair. The
action took some of the intimidation right out of him.
Though he hadn't given her reason to doubt his
agenda on this little assignment of theirs, she'd been
fooled by a pretty face before.

MANHUNT
IN THE NARROWS

NICHOLE SEVERN

Harlequin

INTRIGUE

To Sara A.

Couldn't have written this one without you.

INTRIGUE™

Recycling programs for this product may not exist in your area.

ISBN-13: 978-1-335-69017-3

Manhunt in the Narrows

Copyright © 2025 by Natascha Jaffa

Harlequin Enterprises ULC
22 Adelaide St. West, 41st Floor
Toronto, Ontario M5H 4E3, Canada
www.Harlequin.com

Printed in Lithuania

MIX
Paper | Supporting responsible forestry
FSC® C021394

Nichole Severn writes explosive romantic suspense with strong heroines, heroes who dare challenge them and a hell of a lot of guns. She resides with her very supportive and patient husband, as well as her demon spawn, in Utah. When she's not writing, she's constantly injuring herself running, rock climbing, practicing yoga and snowboarding. She loves hearing from readers through her website, www.nicholesevern.com, and on Facebook at nicholesevern.

Books by Nichole Severn

Harlequin Intrigue

Red Rock Murders

Manhunt in the Narrows

New Mexico Guard Dogs

K-9 Security
K-9 Detection
K-9 Shield
K-9 Guardians
K-9 Confidential
K-9 Justice

Defenders of Battle Mountain

Grave Danger
Dead Giveaway
Dead on Arrival
Presumed Dead
Over Her Dead Body
Dead Again

Visit the Author Profile page at Harlequin.com.

CAST OF CHARACTERS

Sayles Green—The Zion National Park ranger has seen it all. At least, until the FBI wants her to lead a manhunt for a serial killer on one of the park's deadliest trails. It's her duty to protect her charge and keep Agent Broyles alive, but the park she loves and her heart just might be turning against her...

Elias Broyles—The FBI agent has no survival skills. Made all the more apparent as he enlists Zion's most experienced—and intense—park ranger to hunt a killer. It's Sayles job to protect him from the park, but Elias finds himself putting his life—and his heart—on the line for her as the killer closes in.

The Hitchhiker Killer—He's working his way across the country but has found himself cornered in Zion National Park with a ranger and the FBI on his heels.

Chapter One

There were human remains all over the park.

National park ranger Sayles Green leaned into the familiar burn at the back of her quads as she descended past the Emerald Pools trailhead and into the main vein of the park.

Zion National Park could've been considered a wonder of the world with its sheer rock faces and plummeting gorges. Plant life thrived in the middle of the desert where temperatures reached over 110 degrees multiple times throughout the year. It wasn't just cacti and dead things that kept her eyes from itching and her nose from spreading her DNA over every trail and tourist but maple trees, horsetail that looked like failing bamboo, and fuzzy great mullein. Rare. Exquisite. Isolated.

The park was no Grand Canyon, at least not in the sense of how many bodies she and her fellow rangers pulled through the front entrance, but she liked to think that was due to her dedication to protect the park from the people and the people from the park.

Still, there was an off chance the report she'd gotten less than an hour ago from a frantic, glassy-eyed tourist—most likely a victim of the alcohol she'd smelled on his breath—held some weight. Of all the national parks in the United States, Zion had its own reputation for falls from its 5,000-plus-foot cliff faces, for drownings and hypothermia thanks to the 1,000-foot depth of the Virgin River, and for its sheer ability to attract the most egotistical and arrogant hikers on the planet. Because they certainly couldn't die on a simple hike, right?

Sayles followed the man-made bridge over the tail end of the river and into the parking lot on the other side of the main artery that shuttled hikers to any one of eight current open trailheads. The truth was, anyone could die out here. A teen stepping off a cliff edge in the middle of the night looking for a restroom. A child who'd gotten too close to the river's spring rapids and fallen in. A grown man trying to get the perfect angle for a selfie along the park's most dangerous ascent with nothing but a chain handrail between him and a 5,000-foot drop.

She'd seen it all. Grieved it all.

And yet this park—with its dangers and fair share of overpacked trails and stupid mistakes—was all she had left. All she wanted. She protected woods and wildlife from hunters, destructive tourists and the occasional fire. She brought bad guys to justice while maybe even saving a few lives in the process. She'd carried scorpions and rattlesnakes out of campgrounds and her own personal trailer, transported a bighorn sheep to a rehab center, and convinced a bear to get out of a dumpster near the visitors' center. She'd changed flat tires, helped resolve marital disputes, provided directions and managed to extricate dozens of keys locked in cars. Her life as a ranger was as multifaceted as it could get. Freeing. Hers.

Sayles stood in line with the rest of the group waiting for the next shuttle. A couple of kids on leashes dared to strain against their parents' hold under and around the flimsy barriers meant to corral tourists into single-file lines, and she had to check herself from asking whether they'd come with their shots or if that'd been a separate appointment. The sun's heat worked its way beneath her uniform. The button-up short-sleeve shirt and shorts weren't fashionable in any sense of the word, but they got the job done. And that was what she was here to do. A job. The buses came every ten minutes. She didn't have to wait long before the newly christened electric shuttle pulled to the curb.

The driver's radio crackled with a request from the other end as she ascended the two steps at the front of the bus with a nod in greeting. The cell coverage in the canyons was nonexistent most days and unreliable on others. Couldn't take the chance of dropping calls during an emergency evac. She didn't know the shuttle driver's name. Hell, she could barely remember her own most nights as she fell into a dreamless sleep of exhaustion after her shift. That was how she liked it. Drivers, rangers—and their perspective cohorts—maintenance personnel and scientists tended to keep to their own pacts.

Sayles took her seat across from the family with the two children feral enough to require leashes, and the shuttle kicked into gear with a jolt. It didn't take long to hit the next stop. Two minutes, maybe three, before she was descending the bus stairs and dropping onto the sidewalk in front of the Temple of Sinawava trailhead.

Into a land of fishermen.

Hikers trudged across the open grass as though they were wading through several feet of water, sleeved in thick waterproof overalls, heavy rain boots and jackets.

Because that was what was required to gain access to the Narrows—a sixteen-mile combination of rapids, unclimbable sandstone gorges and a maze of death traps. Sayles walked the one mile to the end of the paved riverside walk and was confronted with a crowd gathering at the edge of the Virgin River.

Right where the inebriated tourist had told her to look.

"Park ranger, step aside." She forced her way through a crowd of sweating red faces and odor-heavy shirts. To find a body half submerged in the river's clutches.

Holy hell. Sayles lunged for the man's side and pressed two fingers to his neck. No pulse. She grabbed the radio on her hip and pressed the push-to-talk button. "Risner, come in." It took a few seconds, but the radio gods were looking down on them today, and she managed to get through. Her skin heated underneath her ponytail and iconic ranger hat as she studied the face staring back at her. There was still some color in his cheeks, a touch of warmth despite the freezing temperatures of the river. But he was undeniably dead.

"Go ahead, Green." The district ranger's voice broke on her name. Risner wasn't anything spectacular when it came to the job. By the book, a little bit sexist and a whole lot of bland. But she couldn't do this without him. He'd come on a decade before she'd been hired, but they'd been up for the same promotion a few months ago. She'd gladly passed on rising to district ranger to him. Too much paperwork. He'd have a lot more today.

She surveyed the cluster of onlookers around her and gauged her chances of being able to control them on her own. It wasn't looking good as another shuttle full of hikers ambled down the paved path right toward them.

"I need one of the law enforcement rangers. We've got a body. We have to close access to the Narrows and get everyone off the trail. And you're going to want to get up here. Now."

"What the hell is going on out there?" Risner asked.

"We've got a body." She managed to branch one arm out to keep tourists from getting too close to the scene, but she couldn't do anything to stop them from getting photos and taking video.

Whispers breathed through the mass.

Is he dead?

Wait. Was he killed?

Did he drown?

The same questions tried to break through the barrier of detachment she'd constructed the moment she'd set eyes on the body, but she couldn't give them weight.

"Everyone, please. I'm going to need you to take a step back." Sayles tried to herd them toward the paved path, but it was just like any other day when dealing with people who thought they knew better than a trained professional in the middle of the most dangerous environment on the planet. Negotiating with wild cats. The whispers grew louder. Full panic was about to take hold. Question after question vaulted through the crowd at her, as though she knew all the details of how a body had ended up on her trail. But she'd dealt with far more terrifying circumstances than this. She set her fingers between her lips and whistled above the increasing assault of questions. "Everyone, look here. I'm Ranger Green, and I need you to do exactly as I instruct to ensure you all make it out of the park tonight. Is there anyone who saw what happened?"

Nobody raised their hand.

"Has anyone seen this man before? Maybe on one of the trails or at the visitors' center?" A hand went up in the back. "Great. Come stand by me. Did anyone see or hear anything unusual here on the trailhead or on the trail?"

"I heard a scream. I… I turned around and there he was. Just lying there," a woman said. Her voice betrayed the realization sinking in minute by minute. She'd wrapped her arms around herself as though she were guilty of killing the man herself. A tremor shuttered through her. Shock. She was going into shock. "I didn't know what to do."

"All right. Stand next to me, your arm touching mine. Don't break the contact, understand?" It wasn't much, but it would give the woman something to focus on over the next few minutes. Sayles tried to keep her own voice even and raised it over the nervous and shifting crowd. She'd volunteered for short-haul operations, dangled at the end of a rope from a helicopter during rescues and climbed these cliffs with minimal support. But she'd never faced a body on her own. There had always been another ranger to walk her through the protocols. "Ladies and gentlemen, law enforcement rangers are on their way. We will be closing the Narrows trailhead. I need you all to gather your parties and belongings and make your way to the shuttles where you will be taken to the visitor center and asked for statements."

In her peripheral vision she saw another group had moved up the Riverside path, headed straight for her. Every muscle in her body was prepared to force them to turn around, until she spotted District Ranger Risner in the middle of the group, his gaze locked on her. Then the body. He'd brought the cavalry, and a rush of release coasted through her. It didn't last long. Because along with two other rangers—law enforcement rangers from the look of it—a fourth person compressed the air from her lungs. He stood out, a misfit among the rangers. Taller, more muscular, even outfitted in jeans, boots and a T-shirt. She didn't recognize him. Only men like him. Far too aware of their surroundings. Controlled. On alert for the slightest threat. And if he and any of his partners were in the park...

Sayles's breath lodged in her throat.

"Listen up, folks." Risner's voice rose over the murmurs and complaints. "The shuttles are waiting to take you back to the visitors' center. I apologize for the inconvenience, but please, we need you to leave this area as soon as possible."

Yes, a dead body was certainly an inconvenience.

The man Risner had brought centered his attention on the body at her feet. Barely sparing her a glance. All about the job. Principled and disciplined. Unwavering. She guessed she should be thankful for that focus. Because experience taught her that having that kind of intensity on her would be a very bad thing.

Sayles sidestepped, moving both potential witnesses away from the remains for the law enforcement rangers to do their job. Hopefully she'd be forgotten once she handed them off. "I asked these two hikers to remain behind to give statements."

"Agent Broyles of the FBI, this is Ranger Green." Risner pointed a strong finger toward her. The district ranger's thin, ratlike face contorted into something like a smile. A mask for those who didn't have to deal with his underhanded comments and criticism on a daily basis. "She's going to be the one you want."

That all-too-trustworthy gaze tore from the body at their feet and landed on Sayles. "I hear you're the one who can get me through the Narrows in one piece."

She'd hiked in and out of the Narrows and everything in between every weekend since she'd been hired four years ago. Rain, shine, snow, flood. That last one was far more likely this time of year when the winter snow was melting at an alarming rate. She knew the trail better than anyone else in the park, but panic flared hot in her chest. What the hell was the FBI doing in her park? "Why would you want to do that?"

"Because we have a killer on the loose, Ranger Green." Agent Broyles straightened to his full height, a full head above her. "And I need your help to find him."

Chapter Two

Ranger Green didn't like him one bit.

Elias Broyles faced a collection of national park rangers in Zion's visitors' center of all places, very aware of Green's desire to make him all but invisible. She'd kept her gaze solely honed out the shuttle window the entire ride back. Going out of her way to avoid him, it seemed.

Hikers of all types, from toddlers to overpacked amateurs to leathery, sunbaked mountaineers, had been escorted away a little less than thirty minutes ago. It would take a few hours to ensure visitors cleared out of the nearly 150,000-acre national park, but this couldn't wait.

Despite floor-to-ceiling windows punctured throughout the single-story structure, the scuffed brown cement and exposed support beams urged him to seek out more light. As if the natural woods and tones could close in on him at any time. The half walls showcasing things like Zion's geological layers and something called Weeping Rock didn't help with the open concept his body craved. A ceiling fan over the information desk failed to cool the space, but that was what he got for overdressing.

"Rangers, the FBI is in need of our expertise." Risner hiked his thumbs into his belt and puffed out his chest like one of those birds Elias had seen on the Animal Channel.

Except the man had the uncanny resemblance to a rat with beady dark eyes and a thin face. His skin wasn't as deeply tanned as the rest of his rangers, but the man worked hard to give the impression he'd serve right alongside them in any situation. Truthfully, Elias wasn't sure the man had walked these trails in months. Risner rocked up onto the toes of his boots. "As you know by now, a body was reported by a hiker about an hour ago. Ranger Green responded and called me for assistance. From the look of things it seems to be a case of foul play. Agent Broyles, tell us what you need."

Foul play? Did people still talk like that?

Elias caught sight of Ranger Green's focus from the back row of wooden benches meant for visitors to sit and watch an introductory movie about the park. As far from him as she could get. Captivating, ethereal eyes—the color of rare jade and just as cold—centered on him beneath that iconic ranger hat. She hadn't said a word since his request for assistance back at the death scene. That distance was still firmly between them now, though he couldn't imagine what he'd done to earn her dislike in the hour since he'd stepped into the park. She'd kept a level head after confronting the body. Something he certainly hadn't been able to do his first time in the field. But maybe this wasn't her first time. Or maybe she just didn't like his face. He couldn't do anything about that. Besides, he wasn't here to make friends. He'd come for redemption.

"Rangers, our victim has been identified thanks to the ID in his jacket pocket. As far as we can tell, he was in the wrong place at the wrong time and not specifically targeted by his killer. His remains are now in the possession of your law enforcement unit and are being escorted to the Kane County medical examiner to determine how long ago and how he was killed, but we need more information. That's where you come in. There was a witness at the scene, but we need to know if our victim was traveling or hiking with anyone else in his party and what drew the attention of our killer."

"You just said he wasn't targeted." Ranger Green notched her chin higher, almost daring him to contradict himself to a room full of her colleagues. He had a feeling this wasn't the kind of woman who would back down. "Wouldn't your time be better spent focusing on the person who killed him?"

"You're right. I did say that, but that doesn't mean the killer didn't get something he needed from his victim. Supplies, cell phone, cash—killers need resources to survive here just as much as the rest of us." And they would take advantage of anyone who got in their way. "I want to know why the killer chose this victim over the dozens of others on that trail. As for the person who killed your hiker, my partner and I have been hunting a suspect who has left two bodies in California and one in Nevada. The unsub seems to be sticking to the main freeways, targeting drivers who travel alone, then stealing their vehicles until he runs out of gas before moving on to his next victim. We don't know where he is headed, only that the three victims' cell phone GPS indicates they all stopped on the freeway for a brief time. Most likely to pick up the killer. A vehicle belonging to his last victim was reported parked here at the visitors' center early this morning. My partner is searching the van now."

Risner raised his hand as if they were in the middle of a complicated psych lesson. "Unsub?"

"Unidentified subject." Ranger Green leveled that compelling gaze back on Elias, and his body tightened in all the wrong places. "It means they have no idea who they're looking for. Just that he's leaving a trail of bodies behind him. And now he's somewhere in the park."

It seemed Ranger Green had educated herself in homicide investigations. Interesting. That didn't help keep the atmosphere in the visitors' center from growing frenzied. Rangers looked to one another and kept to low whispers. "While we may not know the killer's identity, Ranger Green managed to secure a witness at the base of the trail who reported seeing the killer shortly after the victim's body was discovered. We've got a basic description of his appearance, but nothing more. It's possible our unsub will try to secure another vehicle, but we have Springdale police and your law enforcement rangers at every entrance to keep him from escaping."

"He went up the Narrows." Confidence bled into Ranger Green's assessment. That kind of intensity was hard to ignore, but he imagined it had caused her a lot of problems here in the park considering how many rangers had put physical distance between themselves and her position in the back row. Not a team player.

"We believe so, yes. A killer's number one priority is survival. He will do whatever it takes to avoid capture and arrest and try to wait us out. Lucky for us, adrenaline tends to make suspects very, very stupid, and I intend to take advantage." Elias folded his arms over his chest. "Problem is we aren't trained for this terrain. I'm going to need a guide to get me up the Narrows safely while my partner takes point here to prevent the killer from leaving the park."

Risner clapped his hands, facing the dozen or so rangers. "I've got the best rangers in the service willing to do whatever it takes to help. Apart from Ranger Green, I'm your best bet, Agent Broyles. Been protecting these trails for over a decade and assisted in a number of rescues. There isn't a single mile of park I haven't hiked."

Ranger Green gathered a khaki-colored pack from near her feet and stood to leave. Slinging it over her shoulder, she didn't bother glancing back as she extricated herself from the group. Making a quick exit for the front of the building when no one else bothered to move.

"I need someone who specifically knows the ins and outs of the Narrows." His brain latched on to the woman who'd extracted herself in a rush. He was trained to assess human behavior, and Ranger Green was trying to take herself out of the equation. Elias forced his attention back to the park's division ranger. "When was the last time you were on the trail?"

"Oh, uh. Well, it's been a while." Risner's nerves got the better of him, sucking the vibrato right from his voice. Yeah, no. Elias couldn't rely on someone who cowered at a hint of "I've been managing my team more these past couple of years."

They'd wasted enough time. Every minute he wasn't on that trail was another opportunity their killer would slip away. Again. Elias faced off with the remaining rangers. "Who here has the most experience in the Narrows?"

"Sayles does," one of the other rangers offered. "She hikes it every weekend like clockwork."

Risner ducked his chin. "Unfortunately, Ranger Green doesn't quite have the experience you'd need for your search, Agent Broyles. She's only been working here a few months."

"I thought you prided yourself on training the best rangers in the National Park Service," Elias said. "If Ranger Green has the most experience on the trail, she's the one I want guiding me during this manhunt."

Risner's jaw worked back and forth before he raised his hands in surrender. "Of course. Whatever the FBI needs. I'll get her for you."

"Not necessary. She just left. I'm sure I can find my way around a parking lot." His words sounded a lot more defensive than he'd meant, but there was something about the district ranger Elias didn't like. He shoved through the visitors' center doors and sucked in a breath at the view. Grand red rock cliffs stood sentinel from every direction, bright orange as midday sun arced overhead. It was enough to remind him how inconsequential a single human was on this planet.

Movement through the half-empty lot caught his eye. There one moment. Gone the next. Elias picked up his pace, ignoring the commotion around a built-out van two rows over as his partner ripped the vehicle apart for evidence. It took less than two minutes to catch up with the woman determined to get as far from him as possible. "Ranger Green, hold up."

She slowed her escape but didn't bother turning to face him. Head tipped back onto her shoulder, she'd obviously hoped to get out of the lot unscathed. Ebony hair cascaded across lean shoulders uniformed in a gray button-up before she confronted him. "Agent Broyles."

The defensiveness in those two words shook him to his

core. "Word is you have the most experience in the Narrows. I'd like you to assist me during this investigation."

She paled at the statement. According to her expression, it most definitely was not a compliment. "There are far more qualified rangers I'm sure are happy to tag along during your search."

"No. There aren't. I need to get up that trail fast without dying, and according to your colleagues, you hike the trail every weekend." He wasn't going to budge. It would be her, or he'd have to hike with Risner. Not exactly his idea of a good time. "You have up-to-date experience I could use to find the man who killed a hiker in your park this morning."

Ranger Green stepped into him, all fury and barely leashed control pinching her eyes at the corners. Even a whole head shorter than him, she stood there as a one-woman army. "Did Risner put you up to this?"

"Excuse me?" He had the urge to step back to avoid whatever hell was about to rain down on him, but he was an FBI agent, for crying out loud. He could handle one little ranger.

"Is this another one of his pranks?" she asked. "To see how far he can push me before I quit? Because I'm telling you right now, it won't work. I'm not going anywhere."

"I have no idea what you're talking about." Though he wanted to know exactly what the district ranger had done to get a rise out of her like this. "I really just don't want to die on that trail, and you seem like the kind of person who can make sure that doesn't happen. Please."

The heat in her expression drained, but Ranger Green didn't add that distance back between them. She looked him up and down, taking in his jeans and T-shirt and tennis shoes. "You're going to need gear and supplies. We'll leave as soon as you're ready."

"You don't like me very much, do you?" His question had nothing to do with this investigation and everything to do with his own curiosity for a woman who clearly anticipated a battle from everyone around her.

"I don't have to like you during your manhunt." Ranger Green headed for a beat-up four-door sedan and tossed her pack inside. "I just have to keep you alive."

Chapter Three

Closing down the park took an act of God.

Or a serial killer on the loose.

Sayles clipped into her custom hydro bib. The water-proof material resembled a pair of overalls apart from one key difference: it added at least ten pounds to her already heavy gear. Worth it. The Narrows was one of the least forgiving trails in Zion. If you could call it a trail at all. Entry started at the bottom and forced hikers to travel upstream directly in the Virgin River anywhere from ankle-deep waters to full-blown you're-going-to-have-to-swim-from-here-on-out. And considering April marked that time of year when the snowbanks started melting, she and Agent Broyles were in for a treat. They could look forward to freezing temperatures and loss of more favorable camping locations ahead.

They had to do this fast.

Speak of the devil himself. She watched as Agent Broyles hauled a backpack over one muscled shoulder, those dark eyes locked on her as he approached from the visitors' center. It was cute the way he thought he'd get through this in jeans and T-shirt. This wasn't one of the park's amateur hikes where parents could carry their toddlers on their shoulders or stop to have a snack.

"Did you get everything on the list?" The answer was plain as day in his chosen outfit. Jeans would soak up river water and weigh him down. Not to mention they wouldn't do a whole lot of good against hypothermia. She could just imagine the blisters from the seams now. She'd left the suggestions for gear and supply with one of the information rangers in the visitors' center. He'd clearly chosen to ignore some of the key components. Probably thought he knew best, but nature didn't work that way, and people had died in the park for that same arrogance.

Agent Broyles unshouldered his bag, setting it down in front of him in the lot. They'd have to take the shuttle back to Temple of Sinawava to access the trailhead, then go on foot from there. And the sooner they got going, the better. She'd caught word of a storm about forty miles out that looked like it had its sights on the park. While she was sure the rest of Springdale police and whoever Agent Broyles had brought along on this hunt could manage their respective search grids in the rain, the Narrows would kill them if it flooded. "Think so. First aid kit, matches and a lighter, water, map, sunscreen, flashlight, knife, some food."

It was a good start. Between the two of them, they could make up the lack wherever needed, but there was one key item missing off that list. "What about a tent?"

She wasn't the sharing type.

"Worried you'll have to bunk with me, Ranger Green?" Amusement lit up his face and corrupted the whole emotionally unavailable law enforcement officer persona he'd had going on in the visitors' center. She wasn't dead. Agent Broyles was more than handsome with high cheekbones, a strong jawline with the barest hint of facial hair, a straight nose with a bump between his eyes that said he'd broken it at least once and a body that would put any Greek god to shame. None of which would be getting within twelve inches of her if she could manage.

Sayles shut down the urge to roll her eyes into the back of her head. Wasn't worth the sparring energy. Not for what they would face ahead. While she could easily traverse the Narrows alone, she wasn't just responsible for herself on this one. If she got a federal agent killed, even as a by-product of his own stupidity, she'd lose…everything. "There are no fires allowed in the park. A tent is the only way you'll keep from freezing when the sun goes down."

Agent Broyles unzipped his pack, showing off the single-person tent crammed inside. Brand new. They were about to find out just how experienced the federal agent was out here in the big wild. She had her bets with the other rangers. They weren't great odds. "This good enough?"

"It'll do." Twisting toward the trunk of her sedan, she pulled another hydro bib—maybe a little too small and definitely not custom-made for his frame—from the confines and tossed it at his feet. "Put this on."

Agent Broyles rolled the hydro bib out, then glanced up at her as she offered a pair of waterproof boots. She'd had to guess his size to borrow them from another ranger. They weren't perfect, but they would work for what they needed. "We going fishing?"

"The Narrows is an upstream hike. There are only a few areas dry enough to camp. Otherwise, we'll be in the river the entire time." She nodded to the gear. "These will keep you dry for the most part and protect you against water toxins."

He fumbled into the waterproof gear and tried to straighten fully, but the hydro bib was obviously cutting into some very vital organs below the waist. "Is this how it's supposed to fit?" His voice had climbed almost an octave.

"Not so much." Her laugh escaped without permission. "Here. Let me help." She stepped into him. Well, damn. She'd already broken her twelve-inch rule. Working the adjustable straps on his chest, she loosened the gear's hold on his manhood. "How's that?"

"I can breathe again." Agent Broyles shot her that crooked smile again. Wasted on her of all people. He grabbed for the rest of his gear after shoving his feet into the boots. "You just happened to have these lying around?"

"Not for you, Agent Broyles." Her ex had been a few inches shorter than Agent Broyles's six four, but there were a few similarities she didn't want to acknowledge between the two of them.

"Elias," he said. "If we're going to be spending the next few hours, possibly days, together, you might as well call me by my first name."

She didn't agree. Naming something humanized it, and she wasn't interested in getting to know him. "Let's get moving. The shuttle is waiting on us."

She didn't bother to check to see if he'd followed. This was his manhunt. She was just the guide, but Sayles couldn't ignore the permanent goose pimples along her neck and arms. The man they were after had already killed five people, including a hiker in this very park. What was to stop him from turning on a park ranger? It was her job to protect Agent Broyles from the park. What guarantee did she have Agent Broyles would protect her apart from his duty?

Sayles boarded the shuttle, one of the new electric ones the park had invested in over the past couple of years. The engine barely grumbled as she took her seat behind the driver and tugged her pack to her chest. A barrier between her and the man sitting across the too-slim aisle from her.

The ride wasn't more than twenty minutes, but those minutes seemed to drag on forever as she focused every ounce of attention out the elongated windows over Agent Broyles's shoulders. Her body swayed as the shuttle's transmission shifted, making her overly aware of his attention centered on her.

"Risner said you were one of his newest rangers." He had to raise his voice over the shuttle's engine despite them being the only passengers on board. "How long have you been at Zion?"

"Five months." Her inexperience wasn't a secret. She was sure the FBI could unearth her personnel files with the snap of a finger.

"Did you always want to become a ranger?" he asked.

What was with the third degree? Narrowing her gaze on him, Sayles worked to shut down whatever expression on her face was telling him she was up for small talk. "Did you always want to be an FBI agent?"

"Ever since I was a kid." Broyles reached overhead to grab on to one of the many stand bars installed throughout the shuttle bus for balance. "But that was probably because I watched too many true-crime shows. You know, like *Dateline*."

"Your parents let you watch *Dateline*?" Damn it. She wasn't supposed to encourage conversation. There was a reason she didn't trust federal types like him. She had to remember that.

"Let me? No." His gaze cut to the driver as he shook his head. "Did I sneak into the living room in the middle of the night and watch TV after they fell asleep to watch that and *Tales from the Crypt*? Absolutely."

"That show gave me nightmares." As a kid, she'd believed that was the worst that could scare her. Then she'd gotten older and seen what real evil looked like. "My degree is in art history. I wanted to work for a museum, curating artwork and building collections, overseeing preservations, that kind of stuff."

She didn't know why she'd told him that. Wasn't even sure if she'd ever told her fellow rangers about that dead dream. Then again, they'd never asked. Not even her roommate, Lila, who everyone accurately nicknamed Ranger Barbie. But working in a national park came with a lot of transition. Rangers moved across the country to get coveted positions and full-time work, which was a lot harder than it looked. The big parks were where everyone wanted to be. Yellowstone. Yosemite. The Grand Canyon. Otherwise known as the crown jewels of the National Park Service, those were the ones that came with bigger animals to protect, more scenery to guard and bad guys waiting to get busted. Rangers had sabotaged, lied and manipulated their way into those assignments. Rangers like Risner. What was the point of getting to know your coworkers who would stab you in your gray-colored back for the opportunity to patrol Denali?

"Why the national park rangers then?" Broyles asked.

To hide. To escape. To finally have the chance to make her own decisions. Zion wasn't just a place for her to work. It was freedom in every sense of the word. Something she'd never had before and certainly not in her marriage. Sayles gripped her pack a bit too tight. "I needed a change."

The driver maneuvered into the semicircle meant to corral shuttles at each trailhead, and Sayles practically bolted for the door. Not like she could escape the federal agent on her heels, but she could sure as hell put more distance between them. She shouldered her pack and headed straight for the asphalt trail she'd hiked this morning.

Only there wouldn't be a body waiting for her on the other side.

At least, she hoped they didn't come across any more. She sensed she'd already be seeing that hiker's face when she closed her eyes tonight. They were well into the afternoon at this point. Shadows seemed to drip down the cliff walls waiting to consume them whole.

Sayles stepped off the asphalt path and headed straight for the canyon mouth towering over 2,000 feet above them with a mere sliver of eight feet of ankle-rolling, algae-covered rocks between them. "The canyon will block the sun for the rest of the day, but we've got about six hours before sunset hits. At that point, we'll need to make camp."

The slosh of water at her back told her he was sticking close. "Think we can make it to a spot and set up for the night in that time?"

"The driest location to camp is two miles in. About an hour and twenty minutes if we stay consistent." Her feet immediately became sluggish in the mere six inches of water fighting them at every chance. They had to move slow to avoid burning out before reaching a sufficient campground. "Problem is we're right in the middle of snowmelt season. The waters here are much deeper than any other time of the year. Your killer picked a hell of a time to flee."

"I'll be sure to mention that when we catch up with him." Broyles's words echoed off the canyon walls. "Back at the visitors' center, you knew what unsub stood for. I take it I'm not the only fan of *Dateline*."

Knowledge of law enforcement protocols and terminology wasn't something she'd ever been interested in. But that was the cost of escaping a murder charge. "Something like that."

Chapter Four

He wasn't sure how far they'd hiked. But his legs felt as though they were on fire.

Up ahead, Ranger Green made the trek look easy, but he'd already tripped, slipped and face-planted over the slimy rocks determined to stop him from going any farther. What the hell kind of nightmare was this? The getup she'd dressed him in hadn't done a damn bit of good on that last fall. Frigid water had worked down the collar and soaked his T-shirt straight through. His fingers had lost feeling a few minutes ago while she navigated him deeper into hell itself. "You really hike this thing every weekend?"

There was a certain confidence she carried he couldn't ignore. Like she'd been made for this place. Otherworldly and stronger than he'd estimated. Wilder than she wanted to admit. Definitely formidable and guarded. "When I'm not on shift."

His boot slipped off another of the small-ass boulders threatening his every step. Water splashed up to his knee that time, and a growl charged through him. What was he doing here? Oh, right. His last case had gone to hell, and his only witness hadn't survived. His supervisory agent had determined Elias could no longer be trusted and sent him on a wild-goose chase. Someone killing travelers along I-15. But damn. He wasn't an outdoorsman. The farthest he'd ever hiked was to the G laid out in white rocks on the mountain edging his hometown in sixth grade. Before everything had fallen apart two months ago, he and his partner, Grant, upended entire weapons dealing organizations, pulled women and children out of sex-trafficking rings and ran cartels into the ground. Now they were chasing a ghost. Because he'd screwed up both of their careers and any chance for promotion.

Couldn't argue with the view, though.

Sayles slowed her pace, then came to a stop atop an oversize flat rock at the river's edge. For him or for herself, he didn't care. He needed a break. The sun barely reached the tips of the canyon walls high above him, and a chill settled across his shoulders. Or maybe it was those intense green eyes assessing him from a few feet away. "You look like you could use a few minutes."

His lungs agreed. He was in shape. Part of the job. But this… This was something else. Muscles he wasn't aware existed protested every step. "How far until the first campsite?"

She swung her pack forward from one shoulder and extracted a metal water bottle. He'd expect nothing less from a national park ranger concerned with keeping her park garbage-free. Taking a swig, she threw him an unexpected smile. "We've only been hiking for twenty minutes."

Elias nearly doubled over at the realization. He checked his watch. Yep. Sure enough. Twenty minutes since they'd entered the trail. "I'm going to die out here, aren't I?"

"Don't worry. There wouldn't be any need for a manhunt. Given these currents, your body would turn up in a few hours." She repackaged her water bottle and zipped up the bag.

Was that a joke? Elias couldn't help but laugh as he dug around for his water bottle, which was plastic and not nearly as large as the one she'd brought, though he'd made sure he'd grabbed the water purification tablets she'd recommended. "Dark humor is your thing. I'll try to remember that."

With all the death and violence he and Grant had seen over the years they'd been partnered together, humor under pressure was something he understood well. It was a way to not let the bad things follow you home at the end of the day. Though you had to play it right. That meant no jokes around superiors or grieving family members. Both rules his partner had ignored a time or two. Maybe their current assignment wasn't Elias's fault after all.

"We've got to keep moving. Radar picked up a storm moving this way." She shrugged back into her pack but waited for him to catch up. "Flash floods are the biggest danger on this trail. The rating was low this morning, but there is a long section of the Narrows we won't be able to escape if we get caught in the rain."

"Good chance of dying. Noted." Elias tried for a thumbs-up. Damn it all to hell, his entire body hurt at this point. "So who'd you have to kill to get gear that fit me? Because I have a feeling you're not the kind to go out of your way to make sure I was prepared today."

"The boots are Risner's," she said. "What he doesn't know won't kill him."

He had to bury the hot thread of annoyance at hearing she had access to the district ranger's personal effects. Wait. "You stole them?"

"Borrowed." She angled her chin over one shoulder, putting him in her peripheral vision. Keeping tabs on him. "Don't worry. He'll get them back after they recover your body."

A seam rubbed the wrong way on the inside of his jeans. Taking off the first few layers of skin. Damn it. Water had made its way to his jeans. This was not going to be pleasant. "And the hydro bib?"

She faced forward, shoulders going tight. "My ex was really into fishing. I took that and the rest of his stuff out of spite."

Okay. So he could add vengeful to the growing list of attributes. A lot like the muscles in his legs screaming at him to go to hell if he took one more step. "I take it the relationship didn't end well."

"Most divorces don't end on good terms." The inflection had drained from her voice.

She'd been married. Why did that fact heat feeling back into his fingertips? Elias followed in her steps, kept to the same slimy rocks, spotted the steady gaps between. There was a method to her madness. As if she was following a map laid out by Indiana Jones himself. Or maybe he wanted to have more confidence in her so they got out of this alive. "I'm sorry. I didn't mean to pry."

"You didn't." An energy he couldn't put his finger on stiffened her movements. "I haven't seen anything to suggest your killer came this way, but we have miles ahead of us, and he has a good hour head start. He could already be at Orderville Canyon Junction. It's where we want to camp tonight."

He didn't miss the change in subject. All right. Back to the reason they were here. He could do that. Elias forced himself back into the right headspace, one focused on the potential of them coming into contact with a serial killer. Rangers had federal jurisdiction, but there was very different training involved between the NPS and the FBI. He was accustomed to violence. Sayles was accustomed to scolding hikers for relieving themselves off cliffsides. "Guys like this will do whatever it takes to escape arrest. Once we find him, I'm going to need you to stay behind me. Use me as a shield if you have to. I go down, you run like hell. Got it?"

"Got it," she said.

No argument. Interesting. He'd expected more of a fight, but he'd give her credit for self-preservation. A lot of people—especially civilians—fantasized about playing hero in situations like theirs. Though rangers weren't civilians in the least. They were federal agents only on a much grander scale. Some, like Risner, let their ego lead the charge, but Elias didn't get that feel from her. She wanted to be small and stay out of the way. Hidden.

They moved a few more yards upstream with nothing but the white noise of the river filling the silence, and damn it, the seam in his jeans cut through the first few layers of skin as easily as a blade at this point. He'd survived far more violent injuries since signing on with the Bureau, but this was a slow death. Heat charged into his face as he realized Sayles had stopped ahead, that intense green gaze on him.

Her eyes pinched at the corners. Assessing him from head to toe. "What's wrong with you?"

"Who says anything is wrong?" He hopped to the next rock and landed without tripping over his own two feet. Hell, maybe he was getting the hang of this trail after all.

"Your face. You keep wincing." She worked her way downstream, closing the distance between them.

"It's nothing." He was a federal agent, for crying out loud. A wet jean seam shouldn't make him feel as though his thigh had caught fire.

Sayles tipped her head back. Clouds rolled above the sliver of canyon overhead. Thick and darker than they should be. She'd mentioned a storm caught on radar before they'd left. Looked like they hadn't managed to outrun it. "We need to pick up the pace. The storm is almost here, and we need to be on higher ground by the time it hits."

Was that him groaning or the river? Elias wasn't sure.

She didn't wait for him to answer, heading back upstream.

Suck it up, Broyles. Wet jeans would not be the reason he met his maker. Every muscle in his legs protested against deepening waters. He wasn't sure he could feel his toes anymore, even with the waterproof boots. The water's temperature rated below freezing, all that snowpack melting off the mountains to the north and into the Virgin River.

A rumble of thunder seemed to shake the canyon around them.

Sayles pulled up short, attention to the sky. Her gaze then locked on him. If he hadn't studied human behavior his entire career, he might've missed the note of panic in her face. She scanned the waters around them, going from clear to muddy in a matter of seconds. What the hell? "Run!"

He didn't need to be told twice. The pain along the inside of his thigh shifted to the back of his mind. Elias forced his body to comply, tucking his thumbs around his pack straps to avoid the bounce. The water fought his every step, working to drag him downstream. He replicated Sayles's footsteps, the areas she steered clear of and her change in direction. Straight ahead to diagonal. To the right.

"Move!" Her warning was drowned out by an angry roar ahead.

His muscles burned harder as the waters seemed to rise several inches in a matter of seconds. Flash flood. The storm must've dumped rain higher up the trail, and now they were going to pay for it.

Panic ticked up his heart rate. At least they'd find his body in a few hours. That was what she'd said, right? It wasn't until Sayles cut down a smaller canyon to the right that hope dared show its ugly face.

She scrambled out of the river's grip and almost straight up a streaked, slippery rock face. Elias couldn't keep up, and she reached back for him as if expecting him to suddenly become a mountaineer. "Come on!"

The roar was growing louder. Closer.

The river water churned around his legs and rose impossibly higher.

Elias latched on to her hand, surprised by the strength behind the tug. He dug his toes into the slick rock and grabbed for the nearest shrub to get hold. His feet left the river a split second before the waters consumed the very rocks he'd been balanced on. But it wasn't enough. The Virgin River was going to eat them alive.

"Climb!" Sayles shouted over the thundering scream of the flood. Pointing to the next hold, she directed him to an outcropping of rocks overhead. His foot slipped. Her hand slapped across the back of his thigh as she took position behind him. Putting herself between him and the river. The waterproof boots weren't meant to be utilized as hiking gear. One wrong move and he'd take her down with him. He had to keep moving.

They'd reached the outcropping, and the ground evened out enough to provide a ledge overlooking the flood. Elias landed on his back, out of breath, staring up at the darkening sky.

The first drops of rain pattered against his face as Sayles centered herself in his vision. "And that's why we don't wear jeans hiking."

Chapter Five

They'd barely managed to escape.

And now she was stuck on a collection of boulders no more than five feet in diameter, marooned over the gushing waters of the Virgin River with a man she didn't know. They'd been lucky. If she and Elias had been even ten feet behind, they wouldn't have survived the crush of the flood.

Agent Broyles, she told herself. Using his first name humanized him.

Rain pelted her ranger's hat and fell in heavy drips from the brim. Her button-up uniform shirt had soaked through, leaking into her hydro bib, and she couldn't stop the chill skating across her shoulders. The sky unloaded its fury straight overhead, but this outcropping had been the only option to stay alive.

Mystery Falls sat off to their right, heavier than usual with the rain. The 110-foot angled rock face wasn't a waterfall in a straightforward sense but smoothed red rock forged over years of drainage. Like the stones peppering the bottom of the river. Thick green trees jutted out from the rock walls in random patterns, but none of them would provide any protection.

Sayles swept her hair out of her face, coming away with

a handful of rainwater as she took a seat. Closer than she wanted to be to Agent Broyles, but there was nowhere else to go, and they were in for the long haul as of right now. "Are you injured?"

"No." He shook his head, droplets flinging every which way, and threaded his hands into his hair. The action took some of the intimidation right out of him. Though he hadn't given her reason to doubt his agenda on this little assignment of theirs, she'd been fooled by a pretty face before.

"Good." She scanned the floodwaters. Dead wood, mud and leaves clustered and broke apart below. The only good to come out of this was knowing the man they were chasing would have to stop his escape to survive these waters, too. If he hadn't already been caught in them. "Because I'm not sure how long we're going to have to stay here. At least a couple hours, I'm guessing."

"Great." Agent Broyles dragged his pack around to his front. "The inside of my thighs could use the break."

She couldn't help but drop her gaze to the topic of this new conversation. Even through the hydro bib, she couldn't deny the strength and muscle encased in waterproof material. She'd gotten only a glimpse while he'd geared up in the visitors' center parking lot, and the image of his toned frame hadn't slipped from her mind since. "What do you mean?"

"About a half a mile back, I tripped. Water got into my gear and soaked a section of my jeans." Agent Broyles ripped his pack open and started searching for something. "The seam feels like it's trying to gnaw through my thigh."

Oh. Okay. A flush heated across her collarbones. Temperatures wouldn't significantly dip until the sun went completely down. They weren't at risk for exposure. Yet. But those chances went up every hour they were stuck. They had to make the most of it now. "That's quite a visual." Sayles unzipped the top of her backpack and collected the packable first aid kit. "Take off your pants."

A stillness she didn't know was possible rippled through him. "I'm sorry. I don't think I heard you right. Did you just tell me to take off my pants?"

"Yes." She'd performed first aid on every manner of visitor to the park from extreme sunburns to overhydration and broken bones. Her training focused more on survival rather than medical, but a few bandages weren't anything she wasn't willing to donate to a good cause. And the way he'd started slowing the last quarter mile or so told her the seams of his jeans were at fault. "I can't bandage your thigh while you're still in your gear, and leaving it to get worse will only slow us down."

"I think I can manage on my own." Was that a matching rush of heat in his neck, or had she imagined it?

Honestly, she wasn't sure why she'd offered to bandage him up in the first place. They weren't friends. They were barely acquaintances, and as soon as this manhunt was finished, they'd never see each other again. She handed off her first aid kit. He had his own, but hers had been customized based on her experience in the park. Larger bandages, for one. His would most likely include the bare minimum and a few Band-Aids. "All right."

Agent Broyles stood, his head instantly connecting with a tree branch. He wasn't able to straighten to his full height. He'd be better off taking off his gear sitting to avoid falling into the river below, but she wasn't about to offer that tidbit of information unless asked.

"There's a tree there." Okay. She was being petty and couldn't hide the smile tugging at the corners of her mouth while she unpacked a deck of waterproof playing cards. She didn't know how long they'd be here. Might as well keep themselves entertained.

"I figured that out. Thank you." He shucked the hydro bib around his ankles. Then went for his jeans. He'd taken the smarter route in keeping his boots on. The second his socks got soaked, he'd be miserable and risk chance of infection. Hesitation slowed him down. "Could you turn around? I wasn't planning on putting myself on display for this field trip."

"No need to be embarrassed about your choice in underwear. We've all been there." Looking up at his lack of answer, she spread the cards in her hand. At a loss of where she was supposed to go. "There's not really any place for me to go on this rock, but if it makes you feel better, I won't look. Believe me, I'd rather be anywhere else."

Sayles angled her head down, but she could just make out his movements in her peripheral vision. First discarding his jeans around his calves, then the shift of muscle higher up. Her heart rate picked up. Breathing becoming shallower. You'd think she was being chased by a bear the way her body heated. If it was possible, she was sure steam would be drifting off her exposed skin at the thought of getting a glimpse of the FBI agent towering over her. Okay. It hadn't been that long since she'd been with a man. Come on.

"Damn it. I can't… I can't get a good look at the damage." Defeat tainted his voice. "I might need your help."

"Might?" Subtext turned out to be the killer of happiness, and she'd given up trying to read between the lines the moment she'd left her marriage. Trying to decipher someone else's meaning, mood and hidden agenda no longer interested her in the least. If Agent Broyles wanted her help, he'd have to ask for it.

"I need your help." He stood strong, feet shoulder-width apart, half-naked and exposed to the rain. She imagined this was not an everyday occurrence, but she couldn't deny the view while she had it.

"Sure." Sayles shoved her playing cards back into the box and rocked forward to her knees. Facing off with the agent's lower body. And what a lower body it was. Tendons and muscle rippled as he was forced to keep his balance in a perfect display of power and strength. Dark hair jerked in place as rain hit the expanse of tan skin. Her mouth dried despite the humidity clinging to every inch of her body, but she somehow convinced her brain to focus on the task at hand.

His tight boxer briefs provided little protection against the constant rubbing of the seam of his jeans between his legs, and the result had taken a few layers of skin off in the short amount of time they'd been hiking. It was one of the reasons she encouraged visitors to choose stretchy, light, soft pantwear, especially during the hotter months. Jeans trapped heat, came with too many seams and got heavier as they collected sweat.

"How bad is it?" Agent Broyles asked.

"Not the worst I've seen, but it's not great." It wasn't just the first few layers of skin that'd been rubbed raw. Blood pooled at the edges, leaving him open to infection if they weren't careful. His attention pressed into the back of her neck from above as she prodded around the four-inch-by-one-inch wound. She could practically feel his body heat radiating into the side of her face. "Oh, were you talking about the mess you made of your thigh or something else?"

His laugh reverberated straight from his mouth into her core. Not the best distraction when she was supposed to be patching him up. "My thigh."

Truth be told, from her current viewpoint, she had no complaints about the status of other...body parts. Everything seemed...great. "I'm going to have to clean the wound and debride some of the skin, but we have to find a way to keep the area dry before I can bandage it."

"Damn," he said. "I forgot my umbrella."

Turning to her pack, she extracted the folded solar blanket and ripped through the bag with her teeth. "Hold this over me and try not to move. No matter how much it hurts."

He unfolded the cellophane, draping it above her head as she'd asked. "Well, you're just a ball of sunshine, aren't you?"

"Not everyone can hike with a wound like this." No. That was not admiration that he'd kept his mouth shut when he'd obviously been in a lot of pain. Injuries turned deadly faster out here than in the real world. But the fact that he'd managed to get as far as they had without slowing them down said something about his character. "You made a stupid decision not to tell me about it sooner. We might not be in this position now."

The solar blanket crinkled above her as he shifted his weight between both feet. "Just add it to the list of stupid decisions I've made lately."

She wasn't sure he'd meant to say that out loud. Sayles managed to get the wound and the surrounding skin dry despite the overbearing storm above. After snapping her hands into latex gloves, she extracted a small pair of scissors from her first aid kit and tweezers to debride the curled and folded skin around the affected site. There wasn't much she could do out here in the middle of nowhere, but it was better than letting it fester. "What other stupid decisions have you made recently? Apart from dragging a ranger with no experience into your federal investigation."

She'd meant it as a joke, but he answered anyway.

"That one I don't regret, considering you currently have the best access to whatever is happening below my belt, which we will never discuss ever again, right?" Agent Broyles didn't wait for her to agree. Good thing, too. She wasn't sure she could keep her end of that deal when it came to unloading crazy stories at the next ranger meeting. "As for the biggest stupid decision? I got myself sent here. Chasing some low-level killer instead of being out there saving the world against the cartels and weapons dealers I usually handle."

"Is that really such a bad thing?" Low-level killer? The man they were chasing had already murdered five people, including a victim in this very park. Didn't bringing him to justice count for something, or was it the power trip that got Agent Broyles's rocks off? A sour taste coated her tongue at the thought. She'd known too many agents like him. Ones who liked to hold that control over others, who served their own agendas despite the promises they'd made. Sayles cleaned his wound as best she could with the alcohol wipes from her kit. Maybe with a little too much force as irritation built behind her sternum.

Agent Broyles hissed at the burn. Good. She didn't know a whole lot about his personal case history, but she knew one thing. Stopping a killer—no matter the bastard's track record—was just as important as all those big fish he preferred. Didn't he see that?

His voice lowered, barely reaching her above the slap of rain against the rock they stood on and the solar blanket overhead. "I got a witness killed."

Chapter Six

The injury wasn't just trying to eat through his thigh anymore.

It'd caught fire.

Ranger Green slapped a clean bandage over the wound, following it up with a couple pats around the edges. Something told him she'd left the alcohol pads on a little too long for a reason. In punishment. "You're done."

"Thanks." Elias tried to fold the solar blanket back into the neat little square it had come in, but it was no use. So he crumpled it in one hand and made quick work of pulling his jeans back into place, then offered it to her.

"You keep it." She repacked her first aid kit and pocketed the latex gloves she'd donned. Pack it in, pack it out. The kit went in next. Seemed everything in her pack had a place, and she wasn't the type of woman to break that habit. "I have another."

Their hot and cold back-and-forth was giving him whiplash. One minute she offered to dress his wound, the next she couldn't even seem to look at him. Like he'd offended her.

The rain's assault had lightened up over the past few minutes, but the river was still too angry for them to get back in it. The only consolation in losing the limited time they had to catch up with their killer was the bastard was just as stuck as they were.

The bandage pulled at the hairs along his thigh as he took his seat again. His knee knocked into hers, and he couldn't help the change in her body language. Too rigid. It only lasted a second, but while his career had taken a nosedive the past couple of months, he hadn't lost his observational skills.

Pulling a yellow deck-size box from her pack, she thumbed through a stack of playing cards. But they didn't look like any normal playing cards he'd seen at the countless convenience stores he and Grant had visited over the past few weeks on the road. No face cards or icons but numbers, bullet points and short paragraphs instead. The pack was color-coded. Blue diamonds, purple spades, red hearts and green clubs with a few black edges for jokers. They each seemed to mean something significant. "What's your poison? I'm really good at go fish."

Elias grabbed the deck from her hands and shuffled through it over his crossed boots. "I tell you I got a witness killed, and you want to play cards?"

"I figured if you wanted to offer the information, you would." A slow rise and fall of her shoulders tried to convince him of her casualness. It was all a lie, though. This woman was anything but casual out here in her element. Constantly aware of her surroundings, scanning the river every few minutes as if looking for something specific. Maybe a body? Always on guard. Especially around him. "It's none of my business why you're here. Just my job to make sure you get out of this canyon."

He kind of liked that. Someone with enough self-awareness to know when to push and when to pull. Why exhaust yourself trying to decipher someone else's moods when putting the responsibility on them to communicate saved everyone time and frustration? He needed more of that in his life. "Fair point."

Elias studied the cards before handing off ten to her. Flipping over the bright yellow-and-orange box they'd come in—thicker than a normal deck—he absorbed the oversize lettering on the front. "The don't die out there deck. Survival tips? Figured you rangers were above resorting to tourist souvenirs for guidance."

"Funny." She took the cards with a little too much force. "I brought them for you, Agent Broyles."

Ouch. Well, he'd walked right into that one. He'd yet to deal his own set of ten for their game—because who the hell actually knew when they were getting off this rock?—and read the first card in his stack. "If you are lost. Keep your cool. Don't panic. Take a break for food and water. Use your map. That's some great advice. For a five-year-old."

"Why do you think I brought them for you?" Ranger Green reshuffled her cards with a wide sardonic smile. Hell, the look fit her perfectly. A little wild and a whole lot daring. Most people had a healthy avoidance of law enforcement. Not overly obvious. Just wary. Like when their nerves get the best of them during a routine traffic stop. She wasn't one of those people. No. Instead, she carried something heavier.

"I see how it is." Elias dealt the cards with the rest of the deck positioned between them. "All right. You want to play, Ranger Green, we'll play. Best of this hand, and when I win, you have to tell me why you don't like me."

Her smile slipped. Barely enough to convince him he hadn't really seen the change. "And if I win?"

"What do you want?" He was far more interested in her answer than he should be. What did a woman like Sayles Green want more than anything? And why the hell did he care?

"If I win, you aren't allowed to speak for the next hour." Those intense green eyes brightened at the idea.

"Wow," he said. "You could've asked for anything, and that's what you're going with?"

"I like my quiet time." She slipped one card free and slid it toward the back of her hand. "It's why I come out here so often, away from everybody else. When I'm not on the trails, it's easier to believe the world isn't as cruel as I remember it being."

The rush of the river filled the silence between them.

Elias shifted his position on the rock beneath them, a very sharp edge working its way into all the wrong places. "All right. Do you have any fives?"

She was forced to give up two cards. And over the next few minutes, his pile grew while hers dwindled. Until he'd collected everything he'd needed to win.

A hint of annoyance flashed in her expression as the outcome took shape. It was a good look on her. The doubt. He wouldn't mind seeing it a few more times before this manhunt was over.

Ranger Green tossed the rest of her cards onto the middle deck. "You cheated."

"I'm not sure it's possible to cheat at go fish." It was, but he wasn't going to tell her that. "Maybe you're just really bad at it. Either way, deal's a deal."

The hard set to her jaw warned him she might back

out, but sooner or later, he would figure out why she'd rather throw herself into that raging river than sit here with him for one more minute. "My ex-husband is a federal agent. FBI, same as you. He worked mostly serial homicide cases. I told you before things didn't end well. It's childish and immature of me to assume you're like him, but I've spent the better part of the past five months avoiding anything and anyone who reminds me of him."

That, he hadn't expected. Elias busied his hands by reshuffling the deck, processing what little she'd given him. He could let her offer more information—as she had concerning his latest admission—but curiosity got the better of him. "That's why you're familiar with case terminology and protocols?"

"No." Her voice shook on that single word. "That came later."

"What'd he do to make you want to divorce him?" he asked.

She didn't answer right away, but they had all the time in the world on this rock. "What makes you think he wasn't the one to leave me?"

"Because you're the one in hiding." He didn't miss the slight widening of her eyes. The mask she wore was good. Probably forged over the years she'd been married. But experience had given him the tools to break through the thickest of lies.

Her breath shook from her. If the temperature had been a few degrees cooler, he was sure he would see crystallized puffs around her mouth. "It doesn't matter. I'm not going to give him the chance to do it again."

That didn't sit well. Elias wasn't sure why, other than an undercurrent of blame that shadowed her words. In his career, he'd met a lot of bad guys. Except sometimes those bad guys convinced everyone around them they were actually good. Had badges and federal credentials and the respect of neighbors, partners and family. He dealt her another ten cards. He'd play as many rounds as it took to bring back that smile from earlier. "Whatever he did, it wasn't your fault."

"You don't know that." She ignored the hand he'd offered, those pretty eyes on him. "You don't know anything about me."

"I know you're running. I know while you do everything you can to convince people otherwise, you're probably scared." He'd seen it enough times during his tenure with the FBI. Hell, even before that. As much as he didn't like to think of his childhood, there'd been days he'd blamed himself for earning that disappointed look on his mother's face. It wasn't that he'd done anything wrong—he knew that now. He'd simply existed, and she couldn't find a way to get rid of him that didn't have her ending up behind bars. If he'd just been good enough, done his homework better, cleaned the house instead of going to his friend's house, maybe—maybe—she could've loved him. It'd taken years for him to realize he'd deserved more than that permanent scowl on her face any time she looked at him. "Anyone who uproots their lives to move to the middle of nowhere and tells themselves the world can't possibly be as cruel as they remember isn't to blame for what happened to them. They're a victim."

She didn't seem to have any response to that. At least not for a few minutes as they quietly exchanged cards in another round of go fish. "The witness you said you got killed. Do you blame yourself for that?"

"Yes." There was no point in denying it. He could practically feel the stain of guilt on his skin. Surprised she couldn't feel it, too, when she'd bandaged his thigh. Elias threw down a card to hand over. "She was a kid, really. No older than twenty-one. A corner boy got shot one night, had his whole stash stolen right out from under him. Problem was, it wasn't his stash. It belonged to the cartel he was running for. Girl had been at the bodega behind him, working the late shift so she could attend classes during the day. Saw the whole thing, could identify the car he drove off in. Smart girl. Had her whole life going for her. My superiors wanted me to let her go. Said we had better ways of getting to the cartel, but I had this feeling she could get us what we needed. She was scared. She was worried the shooter would come back and kill her if she said anything, but I kept pushing. Finally, she agreed. I got her to come in and identify the shooter. Next thing I know, she's the one laid out on the sidewalk. Bullet holes in her chest."

Talking about it didn't do a damn bit of good. No matter how many times he'd told this story, the nightmares wouldn't stop. His hand shook as he discarded the next card. "I pushed her into identifying the killer against my superiors' orders, and the bastard came back to make sure she'd never see court. My mistake lost the FBI the element of surprise. The cartel packed up and vanished, and the man who put a bullet in her disappeared with them. Along with my career."

A hand landed on top of his cards, pulling his attention to Ranger Green's softened expression. No longer guarded by the mask she worked to keep in place. "If you didn't feel guilty, you wouldn't be trying to be better. That's what mistakes are for. To show us what to do next."

His throat worked to argue, but there wasn't anything he could say now that would change the outcome.

The touch was too brief as she extracted her hand, taking the playing cards with her. She repacked and shoved to stand. "The flash flood is over. It's time to move."

Chapter Seven

No signs of their killer.

Sayles gauged her every step as they descended back into the Virgin River. Debris and muddy waters heightened the chances of losing their balance and being washed downstream, but they'd missed their opportunity to turn back. The river reached the middle of her thigh, pushing against the limited energy she had to spare. Clouds hovered over the slice of canyon above, cutting the temperatures even more. The flash flood warning was still too high for her comfort zone, but she'd managed to get them through. It was another mile to Orderville Canyon Junction—the location she intended they'd set up camp. Anything could happen between then and now.

Agent Broyles pushed through as the waters at her back kept rhythm with her steady heart rate. The bandages on his thigh were doing their job, making it easier for him to keep up while staving off infection. He'd surprised her back there. Admitting his mistake in costing a young woman her life. The federal agents she'd known—her husband, his friends and colleagues, all wrapped around her ex's manipulative finger—would've taken a bullet before accepting responsibility for their screwups. Guilt didn't exist in their worlds. But it did in Agent Broyles's. She hadn't expected that.

She supposed not all FBI agents were willing to give false statements, fabricate evidence and commit perjury in the court of law for a friend.

Sayles pushed ahead, maybe a bit too fast for this portion of the trail, as dark memories she'd ignored these past five months caught up with her. It was as if a dam had set up residence in her head. Building, poking, prodding. Every slip cost her a hold on her control, and the bet Agent Broyles had instigated only made it worse. Sooner or later, the dam would break altogether, and not even Zion National Park could save her. Until then, she had to keep it buried so deep she could convince herself that it had been someone else's life instead of hers. "Watch your footing up here. The rocks get smaller, and the flood is making everything else hard to see. Don't need you twisting an ankle."

"You sure you wouldn't want to see that?" He spread his arms wide to keep his balance.

She could hear the smile in his voice but forced herself to keep her attention up front. She had to hand it to him for making it this far. More people than she cared to count failed to survive flash floods. Elias Broyles had found himself three steps back on the ladder of his career, but he was still here. Chasing a killer neither of them was prepared to face at the moment thanks to the flash flood.

The river protested his quickening pace until he caught up with her. His breathing deepened, but he held his own against the current. There were a few rangers who couldn't handle these waters after a flash flood like that. "Kind of seems like you're secretly hoping I slip up."

"That would get you killed." She'd never had an issue keeping her emotions on lockdown around her fellow rangers. Not even Lila, her roommate. The less she revealed about herself, the less chance her ex could use it against her, but Agent Broyles seemed to make it his own personal mission to get under her skin. "Despite your lack of respect for boundaries, I don't want you dead. It's too much paperwork."

His laugh echoed off the red rock reaching for the thunderous sky. "Oh. Is *that* the only thing keeping you from letting me die? Here I thought I'd impressed you with my go fish skills."

How did this man have the ability to draw her away from those angry thoughts she hadn't been able to escape? She hardly knew him, and if she was being honest with herself, she didn't want to know him. It wasn't anything personal. Just the thought of what he represented. What she'd run from. "I'd hate to think of the kind of woman you attract after mentioning those skills on your online dating profile."

"Now, how did you know I have an online dating profile?" He was back to messing with her. Trying to get her to crack. It wouldn't work. It *wasn't* working.

"I didn't until you just confirmed it." Sayles put everything into keeping her attention on the river and not on seeing if his expression matched the amusement in his voice. "But you're the kind of guy who's married to his work. You travel a lot. Doesn't give you a whole lot of time to make personal connections, and the ones you have are short-lived. So you have to rely on online dating profiles or hitting on national park rangers you scam into helping you catch a killer so you aren't spending your nights alone with nobody but your partner and a cold shower. Either way, I can see how you might like the challenge, but I'm betting your online profile says something like: Reasons to date me. One, you'd be the better-looking one in the relationship. And, two, please."

There was that laugh again. Except instead of it bouncing off the red rock around them, it charged straight through her, chasing back the brittle cold sinking through her gear. "How long have you been waiting to use that on me?"

"Since the visitors' center." She kept her smile to herself. Her ability to make him laugh was…new. Though she'd been trying to insult him. She'd always had a sarcastic sense of humor, but it'd bled dry every year she'd stayed with her ex. Felt good to let it out again. And Agent Broyles certainly made the perfect target. "What does your profile actually say?"

"I don't have one. Well, not anymore." Agent Broyles kept his head down. The stain of red climbing his throat gave him away. "Last time I went on a date was around two years ago. We met online. Met up after a few messages. We'd both made it clear we weren't looking for anything serious, but I guess she forgot about that at dinner. She proposed to me in the middle of the restaurant. Had a ring and everything. Not sure how she managed to get my ring size right though."

"Wait. You tried on the ring?" she asked.

"I felt bad that she went through all that trouble." He wasn't laughing anymore. If anything his expression turned outright ashamed. "But, little tip, it turns out, if you accept the ring, you're agreeing to get married. It was all very confusing."

"How did she take it when you told her you didn't want

to get married?" Sayles carved through the next section of trail, the water coming nearly to her waist. The muscles in her legs burned from exertion, but it was one of the best feelings she'd learned to fall in love with since coming to Zion.

"Not well." He shook his head. "Apparently, my behavior wasn't becoming of a federal agent. She called my supervisor and filed a citizen's complaint against me. I still get shit for it."

She couldn't stop the laugh vaulting up her throat. "Serves you right for accepting the ring. You're lucky she didn't follow you home and suffocate you in your sleep."

"I'm aware. Watch out." Agent Broyles latched on to her arm, dragging her against his side as a branch raced straight for her. Automatic and under control, he dropped his hold and pushed forward. "Now I meet women the old-fashioned way. Through thorough background checks and face-to-face interactions on the job."

Her heart hiccupped in her chest. Too distracted by their easygoing banter, she hadn't seen the branch coming for her. The tip of the branch scratched against her hydro bib as it passed, straight across her thigh. Probably wouldn't have done any damage to her gear considering its size, but she had to protect herself and her survival supplies with her life. Only he'd just done it for her. "Thanks."

"Don't mention it," he said. "This is when you try to make me feel better by revealing a far more embarrassing dating story."

Sayles searched the river ahead. No discarded food wrappers or water bottles. No dead bodies or supplies. Seemed their killer was covering his tracks. Had he prepared for this trek before killing his latest victim? "I've only ever dated one person. I ended up marrying him, then I divorced him. Not sure which part is more embarrassing. That I didn't see him for who he really was before I legally tied myself to him, or the fact it took me six years to figure it out."

Agent Broyles seemed to close the distance between them by a few inches. As though she might need his support. "Who was he really?"

"A liar. Manipulative and vengeful." Her throat dried. "I caught him cheating on me. I don't know for how long, but it took me weeks to confront him. I wanted proof, and when I got it, he found out a way to use it against me."

"What do you mean?" he asked.

Exhaustion pulled at her legs. Real or imagined, Sayles didn't know, but she could feel the defeat that came with reliving the past. Its heaviness threatened to pull her under the water's surface, and she was just straight up tired of carrying it around. "I followed him to several locations. Hotels for the most part. At least four of them with four different women over the course of two weeks, but I was too angry to get photos. Every time I saw him it was like he'd stabbed me. I thought we'd had a good life. One we'd built together. I thought we were happy."

He allowed her the space to cut their conversation short or to go on. Sayles wasn't sure she could tell him the rest, but he'd asked for an embarrassing story. This was probably one of the greatest. Nothing but the roar of the river and the colliding debris filled her ears, taking her out of her own head. Distancing herself from those hard-to-manage emotions that came with vulnerability and shame.

"He denied everything. Said I didn't have any proof, and he was right. I didn't. After I confronted him, he left. He was going to stay with a friend for a couple days until

I apologized." She should've known then how much worse it would get. That she was expected to apologize for daring to call him on his adultery. "Two days later, police were at my door. And I was put under arrest."

His hand was on her again, pulling her to a stop. Except she didn't want to look at him. She didn't want him to see her as anything...less. "Under what charges?"

Tremors that had nothing to do with the frigid water temperatures racked her. This was a mistake. She shouldn't have said anything. He'd just made her...feel. It'd been so long since she'd let herself step outside the rules she'd mentally put in place to survive, but she'd been fooled before. He was a federal agent, for crying out loud. She shouldn't trust him, but she had no one else. None of her colleagues, sure as hell not Risner—none of them understood what she'd been through. Sayles brought her gaze to his, expecting the same look she'd witnessed on all of her family's and friend faces when they'd gotten the news. Disappointment. Resentment.

His expression softened. He lightened his grip on her arm. "Sayles."

It was the first time he'd called her by her first name. The shock ricocheted through her chest as if she'd been struck. That single inflection of her name, wrapped in invisible silk and warmth, loosened the death grip her brain had on her. It was almost enough to convince her Agent Broyles was exactly what he seemed. Then again, she'd fallen for that knight-in-shining-armor act once before. She wasn't sure she could survive a second time. "Murder."

A cracking sound split the air. She didn't have time to act as a thick log slammed into her torso.

Then dragged her under the river's surface.

Chapter Eight

It happened so fast.

Elias clawed for something to stop the spinning, but his hands only caught smaller debris as the current tossed him like a dead fish. He had no control. His lungs burned. Freezing water charged up his nose. Mud and cloudy river water kept him from determining which way was up.

It shouldn't be this hard. The water's depth had reached his waist. He should be able to kick to the surface—or at least just stand up—but agonizing seconds stretched as he remained clutched in the river's grasp. His pack worked against him, pulling and keeping him down.

Sayles. Where was Sayles?

She'd been standing right next to him. Elias twisted his torso, tried to pinpoint the sun above him. Only to remember the clouds had rolled in, blocking out the sun and turning the Virgin River into a raging beast.

Pain ignited along one forearm and pulled a silent scream from his chest. Water replaced the last few remnants of oxygen in a rush. But then his boot hit something solid. Dirt kicked up around him. The river bottom. He shoved everything he had into breaking the surface.

The cold burned down his throat as he inhaled greedy gasps. Once. Twice. River water beat against his chest, so much deeper here than when they'd come through the first time. Hell, he didn't recognize this section of the Narrows. He wasn't sure if he was even still on the trail. "Sayles!"

Her name scraped up his throat as a plea. She had to be here. The current would've swept her downstream with him, right? They should be in the same location. "Sayles!"

No answer.

It took more time than it should have to get his feet under him. Stinging pain rippled down his forearm. Damn it. Blood combined with river water and ran in rivulets around his protruding veins and muscles, then dripped into the current. The gash had cut deep, past several layers of skin and into muscle. He'd need stitches, but he couldn't think about that right now. Sayles was out here somewhere. Still under the surface.

Elias shucked his pack free of his shoulders. He couldn't maneuver these waters with it adding to his weight. Hanging it on a thick branch of a tree that looked as though it'd given up the ghost years ago, he faced the river. Searching for something—anything—that gave away her position. "Sayles!"

An average swimmer could hold their breath for a couple minutes. How long had she been underwater? Panic swept away his control as easily as that log that'd pummeled them. His heart rate skyrocketed, breathing going shallow. He could do this. He had to do this. For Sayles.

He dived. The rush of water shocked his nerve endings and nearly stole the breath he'd taken. Leaves and stringy plants clung to his neck and face as he battled the current upstream and blocked his vision. Clouded water strained his eyes, but he wasn't giving up the search. Not until he knew she was safe.

Her uniform and pack blended into the black-and-white world beneath the surface. Nothing to help her stand out against the very forces she'd sworn to protect. Elias surfaced as the burn in his chest became too much. His vision darkened at the edges, and he shook his head back and forth to get a grip. Damn it. Where was she? "Sayles!"

Then he saw it.

The iconic Stetson all national park rangers were required to wear as part of their uniform. It dipped and rose as it came closer. He jumped for it, not daring to let it get away from him as easily as she had. She must've gone under farther upstream. Too far from his current location. Grabbing for his pack, he put what energy he had left into hauling his overworked and tired legs to the edge of the river. His brain told him it'd be faster to get to her in the shallower depths, but he quickly learned there was no shallow portion in this section of the Narrows. "I'm coming. Just hang on."

He hadn't made it more than a few hundred feet before his heart bottomed out. There. A hand shot out to grasp on to the side an oversize log pinning her smaller body under the water's surface. Elias didn't question his instincts, launching himself back into the current. "Sayles!"

Her attempts to pull herself free were slowing every second it took him to get to her in the middle of the river. She couldn't raise her head above the surface. She was drowning right in front of him. "I'm coming!"

He wasn't sure if she could hear him over the rush of her own pulse or the Virgin River's constant roar. Elias buried the urge to throw himself across the log trying to get to her on the other side and rounded the closest end instead. The log had to measure more than twenty feet in height and at least three feet in diameter. It'd lodged itself in a collection of rocks jutting from the river's edge, most of it free of the water. It would take everything he had to lift it, but he didn't have a choice.

Sayles's free hand slapped against the bark. Too slow. She had a minute, maybe less. He widened his stance at the opposite end of the log, secured his hands underneath and lifted as if his life depended on it. The downed tree rolled in his grip and slipped free. Pain stung across his palms, but he'd have to worry about that later. Her hand had stopped moving. He was going to lose her.

He tried again. The log protested as he hefted it off the rocks and let the current take control. The heavy weight rolled straight over her torso before moving onto its initial course downstream, but Sayles didn't surface. His entire body screamed for release as he hiked straight through the current to get to her. "Come on. Come on."

Elias drove his hands beneath the surface, fisting her uniform collar and dragged her up. Her head fell back on her shoulders, skin paler than he remembered. A quick scan of their surroundings didn't give him many options to get her out of the river's grasp apart from the same collection of rocks that'd caught the log. He hauled her frame against his. "Stay with me, Sayles. Almost there."

As gently as he could, he laid her across the rocks and pressed his ear to her chest. She was still alive. Angling her chin into position, he set his interlaced palms over her sternum and administered compressions just as he'd been taught before being allowed to work in the field. Water dripped from the edges of her mouth, but her eyes remained closed. "Breathe. You can do it."

Coughs jerked her torso upward, water spewing across

his chest and face. Green eyes peeled open and scanned the sky before landing on him. Elias turned her onto her side to let gravity do its work on her lungs.

"There you go. Take it easy." Smoothing small circles into her back, he let her take as much time as she needed before sitting up.

"What…happened?" Sayles grabbed for her throat. Most likely to counter the burn clawing up. From what he'd read, the Virgin River was categorized as fresh water, but all the mud and water toxins held opportunity for bacterial infection. She needed medical attention.

"We got railed by a tree." The bruising pain in his ribs told him there'd be marks within the next couple of hours.

"I got stuck." Her memory was intact. Good. They might not have to worry about brain damage, though more than three minutes without oxygen could have lasting effects they couldn't assess here in the middle of the damn park. "My boot…"

"Shhh." He couldn't seem to stop himself from touching her, from making sure she was real, that she'd survived. "You don't have to talk. Just rest. All right? Here." Pulling the metal water bottle from his pack, he offered it. She had water of her own, but his was more accessible.

She took it without hesitation and guzzled a few mouthfuls. Wiping her mouth with the back of her hand—despite her entire body being soaked—she handed it back. Her uniform clung to her in every way, showcasing lean muscle honed from countless hours on these trails. She seemed smaller all of a sudden, that mask of confidence dripping away with the water from her clothing. "You saved me."

"That's what partners are for." He took a few swigs of his own water. "Was I just supposed to watch you drown?"

A shiver rocked through her shoulders. "We need to get dry. The sun will be going down soon, and the longer we're stuck in these clothes, the higher chances we'll start feeling the symptoms of hypothermia."

Another tremor shifted down her back. Could the symptoms already be settling in? Elias didn't want to find out. "Yeah. Okay. Where are we?"

Sayles seemed to realize they'd ended up in a completely different section of the trail than when they'd been hit by that log. Craning her head back, she pointed to the crest of a red rock cliff southeast of their position. Her hand shook, and she quickly brought it back down. She checked her smartwatch. "That's Mountain of Mystery. We passed it about thirty minutes ago. We haven't lost much ground, but almost dying set us back. At this pace, we won't make it to Orderville Canyon Junction before the sun sets."

"That's not good." Trying to navigate these waters when he could see was challenging enough. But losing their limited light? Not to mention dredging through this river without the benefit of the sun's warmth would kill them. At this point their mission to catch up with the Hitchhiker Killer was on hold. All they could think about was survival. Elias scanned the canyon walls on either side of them. "Is there anywhere else we can set up camp for the night?"

She nodded. Nothing more than a couple jerks of her chin. "There's an outcropping of rocks near where we went under, but it's not large enough for two tents, and if there's another flash flood, we'll be caught in the current."

"I trust you, Ranger Green." And for some reason, he meant it. He offered her a hand, noting the cool paleness of her fingers as he helped her to her feet. Her leg shot out to catch her balance, and Elias was right there. First chance he got, he'd take a look at those playing cards of hers and see what the deck said about hypothermia. Because right now, he was pretty sure Sayles was trying to hide the impact of drowning on her body.

"I think we're past formalities, Agent Broyles. You know, considering you saved my life and all. You can call me Sayles." Stepping down off the collection of rocks he'd brought her to, she locked her attention onto her hand. Onto the blood coating it.

"Does that mean you're going to call me Elias?" Damn. He'd forgotten about his arm in the chaos of trying to make sure he didn't have to carry her out of this canyon. Blood seeped into the crevices of his palm and between his fingers.

She didn't answer, closing the distance between the, and grabbed for his arm. Her thumb slipped over his pulse point before she angled one arm free from her pack. Keeping her fingers wrapped around his wrist, she unpacked her first aid kit one-handed. "This is going to need stitches, but we don't have long before we lose the small amount of light left. I'm going to wrap it for now. Once we reach the outcropping, I can put you back together."

"Like Humpty Dumpty?" His attempt to lighten the mood was lost in the glazed film overtaking the green in her eyes.

She circled long strips of medical gauze around his forearm before repacking her kit and heading back upstream. Minutes—was it an hour?—passed in silence as before as they charged for a dry section of rock a mere few feet above the river's surface. "This is where we'll camp tonight."

"Looks like you got your wish." Elias sized up the slightly uneven elongated rectangle of rock two of them were meant to sleep on tonight. "We're going to be sharing."

Chapter Nine

She couldn't stop shaking.

Sayles had changed out of her wet clothing with her back to the FBI agent invading her one-person tent, but she'd lost all sense of embarrassment as she'd forgotten how to ask him for the hand warmers she'd packed. Dry gear hadn't made a difference. Her head felt as though it'd been split down the middle with the effort of trying to keep her teeth from chattering. She was getting worse. Her joints ached, not just stiff from the impact of the log that'd tried to kill her but from the uncontrollable shivers racking her. The pulse at the base of her neck wasn't normal. Too elevated. Breathing too shallow.

And Elias... Concern had etched into his expression a long time ago and hadn't slipped since. He'd taken the lead in getting the tent set up and unrolling their sleeping bags. There was barely enough space for the Mylar material let alone two bodies, but what annoyed her more was the fact that she'd missed the log's approach at all. She'd put them in this situation, and she didn't want his concern. She'd put their lives at risk, but she would be the only one to pay the price. She'd make sure of it.

"Are...you shivering, too?" Hell. She sounded out of it even to her own ears. She just wanted to sleep but knew how slim the chances were of waking up in the morning if she closed her eyes now. "Or dizzy?"

"No." He'd changed into dry gear after helping her out of her wet clothes and boots. The sun had gone down over an hour ago, leaving them with nothing but a single flashlight beam. They'd save the batteries of the second by limiting their resources for now. "You gotta tell me what to do, Sayles. Please."

"I'm...fine." She wasn't fine. Her desperation to take care of herself—to make her own choices and be in control of her own body—was winning out over simple survival. Stupid. She was being stupid risking her lift like this. For what? So another man didn't have leverage to use against her? How would that happen if she was dead? Sayles's let her eyes drift closed. She was so tired. "I'm already...warming up. I just need...to rest."

"All right. If you're not going to tell me how to help, I'll figure it out myself." He dragged her pack into his lap and started removing everything she'd meticulously organized.

She forced her eyes open. "What...are you...doing?"

"Looking for those cards. The ones with survival tips on them." Pulling the slim yellow box free of her pack, he shuffled through the contents until he landed on the red heart cards. "Seek shelter. Done. Replace wet clothing, especially socks. Did that. Insulate from the ground. Sleeping bag takes care of that. Eat carbohydrates and drink an electrolyte solution. Great."

He didn't wait for her permission to dig through the rest of her gear. In seconds, he produced a peanut butter and jelly sandwich she'd made before leaving the visitors' center and an electrolyte mix. "Eat."

Nausea twisted in her gut. "I'm not…hungry."

"Card says you have to eat carbs. Bread is carbs. Eat." He wiggled the sandwich in front of her until she grabbed for it just to get it out of her face.

The first two bites sank to the pit of her stomach and remained there. The next few went down a little easier as he handed off her metal water bottle with the electrolyte mix. Within minutes, the fog in her brain started dissipating. Okay. Maybe there was something to those cards after all.

Elias went back to reading off steps to treat hypothermia. "Use chemical hot pads in armpits and sides of chest." More of her supplies hit the bottom of her sleeping bag as he dug for the hand and foot warmers she'd stashed.

"Between…the thighs." The cards gave good advice, but she was a ranger. In the past five months, she'd seen more people die than on the news from small mistakes rather than big ones. Not utilizing the femoral artery to reverse hypothermia was one of them. "Bigger arteries… pump faster."

"Okay. Let's do both." He cracked the hand and foot warmers and shook them to ignite the heat inside. Like a glow stick. Only this was one that could save her life. "For the record, I'm only feeling you up to save your life."

Her smile pulled at chapped lips. "I won't file…charges."

"Glad we're on the same page." Elias tugged her the sleeping bag she'd cocooned herself inside and slipped calloused hands along the front of her body.

She parted her knees for him and pinched the warmer between her legs as he got it into position. Her heart did the rest, pumping the new source of heat into her veins and throughout her body. Elias kept to the plan and positioned two more hand warmers in both of her armpits. Immediate warmth cascaded through her. And not just from the addition of the warmers. "Thank you."

"Hey, you're not slurring your words together. Progress." His thumbs-up broke the tension. "Looks like I'm better at this survival stuff than I thought."

"I wouldn't go that far." She snuggled deeper into the sleeping bag. The heaviness of the day—and nearly meeting her creator—pinned her in place, but she couldn't deny the sense of…safety she felt having Elias here. He'd pulled her from the river. Had administered CPR. He'd bulldozed through her pride to save her life, and she wouldn't be here without him. Despite his chosen profession and the air of superiority she'd assigned him when they'd first met, he'd done nothing but ensure the success of this assignment. "Don't forget. I was the one to patch up your thigh because you wore jeans on an in-stream hike."

His laugh was softer than the times she'd heard it before. Soothing. "How are you feeling now?"

"Mmmm?" She must've drifted off for a second because she was peeling her eyes open to look at him. The shivers had settled. Her fingers and toes would take longer to recover feeling, but she could finally think clearly. "Better. The warmers are doing a marvelous job."

"Good." Elias grabbed her gear, repacking everything he'd extracted from her pack. She couldn't even get her ex-husband to pick up his dirty socks off the floor. No matter how many times she'd asked.

"Why aren't you feeling symptoms?" It wasn't fair. They'd both gone under. Though she might've been exposed to the frigid waters longer. "Shouldn't you be wrapped up shivering your ass off, too?"

"I have more insulation." He slapped his stomach twice. Followed by that brilliant smile that didn't see the light of day—or flashlight—often.

"Now you're just complimenting yourself. There isn't a single ounce of fat on you." She liked this. The ease between them. In the few short hours they'd been partnered together, she'd dropped the mask she'd donned to stay small and unnoticeable to everyone around her. It felt... good. Freeing. The truth was she didn't have the energy to put it back in place, and wasn't that why she'd come all the way to southern Utah? For the freedom it provided? Only now, she realized, she'd done exactly as she always had. Becoming the person she thought she needed to be to accommodate others. For Risner, her fellow rangers, for Elias. It was all so exhausting.

There was that laugh again, and her body temperature rose another degree from the effect. "You say that now. Wait until you're sweating from sleeping next to me."

After setting their packs at one end of the tent, he secured the front zipper of the enclosure before positioning himself along her back. Hints of his natural scent—mixed with river water—tickled her nose. Something earthy. Then again, she smelled like mud and water, too. There was no escape out here in the middle of the desert. Her breath shuddered out of her as Elias shifted his hips against hers.

"What are you doing?" Panic spiked her voice.

"Those hand and foot warmers aren't going to last more than an hour, and you're still suffering from hypothermia symptoms." He dragged the edge of her sleeping bags higher, under her neck. "I'm here to make sure you stay warm."

"By crawling into my sleeping bag?" Okay. Yes. Sharing body heat was shown to drastically help with regulating body temperature, but the last time she'd let someone get this close, it was her ex. Heat that had nothing to do with the warmers or his body stirred low in her belly.

"You got a better idea?" He shook against her. And not in laughter.

Had he lied about feeling the effects of the freezing temps? Sayles craned her head over her shoulder, putting him in her line of sight. His gauzed forearm threaded over her rib cage and pulled her closer, cutting off her inhale. "Your arm needs stitches."

"Go to sleep, Sayles." Elias set his head against his biceps. Completely at peace while she was anything but. "We can deal with it in the morning."

He was putting her need for rest above his need for medical attention, and she didn't know what to do with that information. If she was being honest with herself, she wasn't sure she could sew in a straight line right now. She'd probably end up butchering any chance of a neat scar. He probably knew that. Knew she wasn't at 100 percent and didn't want to risk his annoyingly good looks on a hack job. "Don't bleed on me."

"I'll try to keep my blood where it belongs." His chest rumbled through her back. The soft rocking helped release the tension in her aching joints, and she felt herself relax against him.

His arm secured around her, as if Elias couldn't stand any sort of distance between them. She didn't have the energy to fight for those precious few inches of air, but that didn't mean she trusted him. "Did you know him?"

"Who?" His voice graveled this close to sleep. The effect did something to her insides.

"My ex-husband." Her pulse slowly receded from the rafters. The few things he'd done—making her eat, drink and warm up—were doing the job. Five months of hiding—of healing—she'd kept herself in check. Wouldn't let herself think of the pain and betrayal and *rage* that came with reliving the past. But in a matter of hours, Elias had pulled it all to the surface.

His arm tightened around her middle. "No."

She hadn't realized she'd been holding her breath for his answer. Sweat beaded at the base of her neck. Within minutes, he'd managed to chase back the cold, and she found herself wanting to lean more into it. Into him. "Oh."

"We didn't finish our conversation from earlier." His whisper sent tendrils of breath across the back of her neck.

"You mean when we were plowed over by a log?" Her ribs still hurt. She wouldn't be surprised to find her body covered with bruises in the morning. If they made it until the sun rose. Another freak storm and they'd be washed down this river all over again. Only with no escape from the tent and nothing to hold on to but each other.

"He had you arrested for murder." Hints of anger stained his voice. Or had she imagined it? "Whose?"

She could still feel the pinch of the cuffs as two officers had placed her under arrest. Sayles stopped herself from rubbing at the healed skin, afraid to lose herself to the fear all over again. But that didn't happen. The heat at her back refused to let her slip from this moment, and she clung to it with everything she had left as she lost the battle to her exhaustion. "His."

Chapter Ten

He breathed through a face full of hair.

The weight crushing his chest wasn't normal, and Elias blinked against the soft light coming through the canvas protecting them from the outside elements. He blew long dark hair off his mouth, realizing the weight belonged to the woman passed out on top of him. She'd escaped her sleeping bag sometime in the middle of the night and invited herself into his.

The hand and foot warmers lay around them. Discarded in favor of his body heat. Elias settled onto his back, not sure what to do next. The sun was up, and if they had light, so did the killer. They had to get moving. "Sayles."

A moan slipped free of her throat, and she buried her face deeper against his chest. Wetness pooled against his shirt directly beneath her mouth. How long ago had she climbed on top of him? And why wasn't he inclined to maneuver her back to her side of the tent?

Oh. Maybe because the last time he'd considered getting close to a woman, she'd asked him to marry her on the first date. But this one was off-limits. While they didn't work for the same agency, they were partners. And he had no inclination to climb into a single-person tent with Grant. As soon as they caught up with the Hitchhiker Killer, he and Sayles would part ways. She'd stay here in Zion, and he'd get sent back into the field on a new assignment. Apart from that, she had a deep-seated hatred of the FBI thanks to her bastard of an ex, and he wasn't excited about the possibility of being suffocated in his sleep.

Who the hell ever thought the woman in his arms was capable of murder? Elias shook her small frame gently. "Sayles."

Another moan—more frustrated—filled the tent. "Five more minutes."

Yep. She wasn't aware she'd climbed him like a tree. "Sayles."

Her head shot off his chest. It took a moment for her gaze to clear enough to recognize the position she'd put them in. Swiping at her mouth, she shoved against his chest to put as much distance between them as possible. Except there really wasn't anywhere else for her to go. The tent had been made for a single person. It was a miracle they hadn't tipped it moving around in the middle of the night. "This is your fault."

"Oh? I'm pretty sure I wasn't the one playing musical sleeping bags in the middle of the night." The instant loss of her heat gutted him, and he wanted nothing more than to drag her back. But they had a job to do. "Though I can't say I didn't enjoy it."

Her face heated, which was a vast improvement over the blue tint it'd taken on after he'd pulled her from the river yesterday afternoon. Sayles extracted herself from his sleeping bag and shoved to stand. Her head hit the top of the tent. "Pig."

"Blanket hog." He swallowed the laugh aching for release as she shot him a look that would certainly put a less confident man in the grave. Elias didn't waste time waiting for her instructions and slipped free of the too-hot cocoon. Grabbing for his pack, he pulled his water bottle free and finished off the contents, then shoved two protein bars down his throat. They were already trying to make up for lost time to catch up to the killer. Any more mistakes and the bastard would escape. "Does the end of this trail lead anywhere else?"

Sayles bit down on the toothbrush in her mouth as she pulled her slightly curly and frizzed hair into a ponytail between her shoulder blades. The shirt she'd changed into last night engulfed her from shoulder to mid-thigh, her sweats at least one size too big. Choosing comfort over style. He liked that. "The Narrows trail officially ends at Big Spring, about three miles from here."

"And unofficially?" Elias folded his sleeping bag in half and rolled it as tight as his Boy Scout leaders had taught him as a kid. It'd been a pain in the ass then, and it was sure as hell a pain in the ass now, but he saw the merit in keeping his gear accessible and organized after nearly getting washed downriver.

Sayles dropped to her knees, dragging her pack closer. She went for the front pocket and pulled a thin brochure from inside. A detailed map of the Narrows. Leaning into him, she ran her finger along the switchback-like trail. "This is us at Mountain of Mystery." She pointed to a section that looked more like a contorted *S* than a trail, then slid upward to the top of the foldable map. "The river continues north with several branches leading west."

Elias made a mental note of each landmark and the *No Flash Flood Escape* warnings peppered up its length. "All right. Is it possible the guy we're hunting can escape the trail off the beaten path?"

"If he knows the area." Handing off the map, she pulled a couple more supplies from her pack, including a fresh uniform. She scrubbed at her teeth as though punishing them for making the decision to crawl into his sleeping bag. "If he doesn't, I can't imagine he'll last long in the backcountry on his own. Some people spend years training to survive out there, rangers included, but most have no clue what kinds of threats are out there. It's one of the reasons all national parks require permits and gear lists. People have died from exposure, animal attacks, starvation. You name it."

The Hitchhiker Killer—it was just easier to give him a moniker than keep referring to him as their killer or the guy they were hunting—had murdered a hiker at the base of the trail. But why? What had made him a target? He could only think of one motive: supplies. Which could mean they'd underestimated his knowledge of the park and the killer's experience. "Can I borrow your radio? I need to get in touch with my partner."

"The canyon blocks radio signals." She swallowed the toothpaste in her mouth, washing it down with water from her bottle. "We'd have to hike pretty high to get through."

"Are there any open areas a signal might reach the visitors' center?" They had to know what they were dealing with. A man relying on his survival brain or a methodical killer who'd chosen this trail for a reason. Time could tell them, but Elias was never one to jump without a plan. And he had Sayles to worry about. If anything happened to her… No. He couldn't let himself get worked up about nonexistent scenarios. That was how mistakes were made.

"Not for another couple of miles. The trail reaches around 5,600 feet in elevation once we hit Wynopits Mountain." Storing her toothbrush, she closed the distance between them, crouching at his side. Her hair slid over her shoulder and brushed against his arm. Raising goose bumps in its wake. She turned the map in his lap, fingers grazing his sweats, and he was instantly reminded of her body pressed up against his chest when he woke. Craving shot through him. Want. "There's a chance we may be able to get something if he hikes high enough there, but it's two miles north. It'll take time."

Time they didn't have for a detour.

"We need to assume whatever reason the killer targeted your hiker was to get extra supplies." Elias refolded her map and took the liberty of reaching around her to slip it back into the same pocket she'd found it. "I'm starting to think Zion was his escape plan all along."

Confusion drew her eyebrows over the bridge of her nose. Over her map or their proximity, he wasn't sure. "What makes you say that?"

"How many people would you say can survive a surprise flash flood and live to tell the tale?" he asked. "I'm pretty sure we would've seen a body by now if he'd gotten caught in that storm."

"Very few. Especially if they've never experienced one before or know the signs on an impending flood." Sayles stared at him, her eyes widening slightly. "You think he's using the park to stop you and your partner from catching him."

"It's not the dumbest idea." Though the Hitchhiker Killer had already killed four motorists and a hiker. What was a couple FBI agents added to the tally? "I'm sure you can tell I have no idea what I'm doing out here."

She shoved to stand, turning her back to him as she stripped out of her oversize shirt. Muscle flexed around her bare rib cage and between her shoulders. Flawless skin, peppered with just a few moles here and there, surged a wave of heat through his chest, and Elias turned away to give her some semblance of privacy. A good amount of color had come back into her skin. No signs of hypothermia hanging around her face and lips. "But he had to have known NPS would get involved, and we *do* know what we're doing."

He'd been lucky. If he'd found her a mere minute later... He swallowed that thought with a tendril of acid.

"Good point." So where did that leave them? Pursuing an amateur or a far more dangerous criminal? What were they headed into? Elias made quick work of changing his shirt, back facing Sayles, and repacking his gear. His head brushed the top of the tent for the hundredth time. He'd forgo the jeans today, opting for the sweats he'd slept in last night. They didn't have time for him to hold them back. Clawing from the almost claustrophobic one-person tent, he grabbed for the clothing he'd hung to dry outside while Sayles had changed out of her wet uniform and rolled them into manageable pieces. His boots had dried. Less chance of more blisters.

Sayles pulled her first aid kit from her pack as she stepped onto the thin, rectangular rock that'd kept them dry last night. "I need to change your bandage before we go."

He had an argument ready but remembered he hadn't been able to get a good visual of the wound along his inner thigh. Which meant exposing himself—boxer briefs and all—to her again. "Yeah, sure."

The ranger seemed to make an effort to avoid looking at him directly, focusing instead on a fresh section of gauze and medical tape. The hairs on his thigh protested as she pulled at the tape already in place, but her touch soothed the stinging almost as quickly as it'd arrived. Despite the hard exterior she presented to the world, she swapped out his bandage with consideration and a care he hadn't expected. "I'm done."

Her coyness was cute but unnecessary. He wanted that fire back, the one that gave him reason to laugh and kept him guessing what she'd do next.

"Stop looking at me like anything has changed between us. It hasn't." She broke down the tent in a matter of seconds, wrangling it back into its packable form. Practiced, with a swiftness he couldn't help but admire.

"If you say so." Elias hauled his pack over his shoulders.

In less than ten minutes, they'd cleared their impromptu campsite and geared up. Sayles took the lead stepping back into the Virgin River's depths. "Mystery Corridor is around this next bend. There won't be any flash flood escape for about a quarter mile. I'm not seeing any incoming storms that would put us in danger for now, but we need to keep the possibility in mind at all times."

Cold worked through his boots and hydro bib—colder than yesterday's temperatures—but he remained dry thanks to Sayles's gear recommendations. "Would you tell me if you did?"

"I'd consider it, but only after reminding myself the paperwork wasn't worth it." There she was. The woman who fought like hell to hold her ground and remind people what she was capable of. Her attention locked on something ahead. A flash of red in a brown, green and white landscape. "You see that?"

Elias didn't hesitate, hauling himself to the center of the river to grab whatever'd escaped downstream. He caught it at the last second and brought the lightweight material back to her position. "What is it?"

"It's a dry sack. Something campers use to keep their gear waterproof." She took it from him, turning it over, then raised her gaze upstream. "This river moves around seven miles an hour, which means someone dropped this recently. Looks like your killer might be alive, after all."

Chapter Eleven

The killer couldn't be that far ahead.

Sayles ignored the exhausted burn in her legs, pushing one foot in front of the other. They hadn't made it far but already she could feel the intensity of Elias's attention between her shoulder blades. The same sensation she'd experienced when she'd woken on his chest this morning.

Her body had absorbed his warmth more efficiently than that of the hand and toe warmers, and for the first time in…a long time she'd slept through the night. No panicking sense of survival. No urge to reach for the multipurpose tool she kept stashed under her pillow. She didn't even remember dreaming. The same sense of freedom she found on the trails these past few months had filled the tent last night. And she was already craving more. Stupid. Stupid. Stupid.

It wasn't because of him. No. It'd been the stress of chasing after a killer. That was all this was. She'd been exhausted. She'd survived drowning, and her body had crashed the moment she'd let it. Elias Broyles had nothing to do with it. Well, except for the fact that he'd kept her from drowning and the effects of hypothermia.

"So are we going to be completely awkward around each other now, or are you just not a morning person?"

Elias's shift through the water hadn't stumbled or slowed in the past thirty minutes since they'd left their small island of rock. The gauze and medical tape was doing its job.

Sayles closed her eyes against that calming balm of his voice. How did he do that? What the hell kind of witchcraft convinced her nervous system he was safe? Nobody else had managed to get under her skin since she'd escaped to Zion, especially not Risner. Not that she was interested in him or any other man, but a woman couldn't isolate herself—or her libido—forever. Her heart rate descended as though she'd sunk into a hot bath, and she gripped her pack straps tighter. "I'm usually on the trails when the sun comes up."

"Awkward it is." His laugh surrounded her, closed in by the canyon walls until there was no escape for its effects. Damn him and his voodoo. "You don't have anything to be embarrassed about. So you cuddled your sworn enemy in the tent last night. I'm sure you were just looking for a heat source last night when the warmers stopped working."

A flare of prickling cascaded across the back of her neck, almost pulling her to a stop. If she turned around, she might shove him into the river, and that was not very ranger-like. "It's awfully presumptuous of you to believe you made the list of people I consider enemies."

"There's a list?" His resulting smile bled into his voice.

Detach. Detach. Detach. She didn't like him—didn't like what he stood for—and had no reason to trust him. No reason to smile back. But her mind supplied the retort and made the decision for her. Traitor. "There is. And you're slowly working your way to the top."

"Who do I have to beat out on this list?" This was

a game to him, and she couldn't help but fall right into Elias's hands. It was the distraction she hadn't expected to enjoy. "Ex-husband? Wait, no. That's a hard position to hold on to if you're dead."

Sayles craned her head over one shoulder to put the agent in her sights. "Who says he's dead?"

"I imagine a lot of people, considering you were arrested for his murder." He picked up his pace to keep in stride with her, slightly deeper into the river at her right. "Unless… He faked his murder just to have you arrested. How?"

Was she really doing this? Trusting a man like Elias with the secrets she'd held on to all this time. For what? Because he made her laugh? Because her body was convinced of the safety he radiated? She'd fallen for that once before.

Her ex had been everything she'd ever wanted. They'd dated for years during high school and college. He'd convinced her and her family he'd love and take care of her forever. But the moment she'd said "I do," everything had changed. The man behind the mask had started appearing in small ways at first. Commenting on her clothing choices, suggesting she avoid that second lemon bar. Bypassing her password on her phone to look something up when he had a perfectly good device provided by the government. The control had only tightened from there. Banning her from reaching out to her parents to apologize after a particularly hateful fight at the last family dinner ended in tears. Detailing who she was allowed to text, what she was allowed to wear, portioning meals, watching what she spent. No more coffee dates with friends. No more movie nights with her sisters. No more going to school. Sure as hell no more contact with male colleagues or friends. She didn't need to finish her art history degree when he was more than capable of providing for their every need.

For years, the noose tightened around her neck. Inch by inch, and she hadn't even noticed. At least, not until it'd been too late. That was when the calls started. The ones he answered in the middle of the night and left their bed to take. When he started coming home later and later. Working a case, he'd told her. He couldn't talk about it. Lies. All of it had been a lie she'd voluntarily swallowed to avoid facing the hard truth.

In the end, she'd been the one to pay the price for his crimes. Still was.

"He had help." Sayles diverted her gaze above, distracting herself from the tightness in her chest, to the dark cloud that'd slipped overhead without her notice. It was heavy and gray. Full of dangerous potential that could force them to go back. "Friends he recruited from his office."

"You mean federal agents." Elias's words barely registered over the lighter crash of falling water as they approached one of the seasonal waterfalls—in full effect—ahead.

The 200-foot cascade was tucked in a small branching canyon off the main trail and created a trail in its wake, silencing the torturous memories in her head. This. This was why she'd fallen in love with Zion, why she'd applied to become a ranger with no experience, no outdoor skills and meager survival know-how. But she'd been a fast learner. From the very first time she'd stepped into the Narrows, she was reminded of the woman she used to be.

The one who trusted herself, who had goals and dreams, who'd figured out the solution to any problem. Staring at this waterfall, she'd remembered who she'd been before her ex had taken over. Strong but a little bit wild. Carefree yet caring for those who deserved her love. From mere minutes of studying this exact waterfall, something had clicked into place. She'd become obsessed, learned everything she could about the park and the skills needed to become a ranger in a matter of weeks. She still wasn't sure why Risner had offered her the job based off her nonexistent résumé, but she would always be thankful he'd given her the opportunity. Even if it meant suffering through his pitiful attempts to raise the bar on sexist pigs.

"We can rest here for a couple minutes." Her body relaxed into that space where the past didn't exist and all that mattered was the next step forward as she splayed her hand into the waterfall. Cold water slapped into her palm, kept her from disappearing completely. "My ex was very good at reading people. Always seemed to know the exact right thing to say. He could win any argument, despite evidence contrary to his perspective. If he hadn't made a career with the FBI, I think he might've been a great lawyer in another life. I think it's how he was able to convince so many people that he was the victim in our relationship. That he was being emotionally abused and isolated and controlled. Not the other way around."

Elias stepped up into her, unaware or unconcerned with the spray of water coming off the rocks. "The police had to have something on you to show a history of abuse."

"They did. Turns out those friends I thought could see what he was doing to me—people I'd invited into our home for dinners and holidays and barbecues—had provided testimony on my ex's behalf." Her stomach soured. They'd been her friends, too. Once. Only now she realized just how deep her ex had his claws in them. "The GPS in my car told police I'd been following him to those motels where he met up with women, keeping track of who he was with. There were texts sent from my phone to his colleagues but later deleted showing how much control I had over his life. He lied to his partner about arguments and punishments and financial abuse I held over him. But it was all a lie."

"But you were the one being abused," he said.

"Not physically. He never hit me, but some scars aren't visible." Sayles pulled her hand free from the crashing water. Back to reality. Back to chasing a ghost in hopes of keeping him from hurting anyone else. "I'd wanted out. A few days before I was arrested, I asked for a divorce, and in return, he faked his death."

"That kind of planning takes time." Elias didn't retreat from the waterfall, squinting up at the source 200 feet up. His expression relaxed as if he were soaking up every moment, memorizing it, enjoying it. In the short amount of time they'd been partnered, she hadn't seen him look so… free. Very unlike an FBI agent who might turn on her, and something released from around her rib cage. "You can't just frame someone in a day. Or without a body."

She'd figured that out while sitting in a jail cell. Somehow her husband had known her intentions. Or maybe he'd just always had an escape plan designed for moments he didn't get what he wanted. She'd never know. Sayles directed her attention back to the main part of the river. "No. You can't. Somehow, my ex had gotten a hold of a body roughly the same size and weight as him. It'd been…

burned beyond recognition, but his wedding ring, the one I'd had engraved for him, was recovered with the remains. Neither fingerprints nor DNA could be recovered to make a positive identification, and the teeth had been damaged. Based on his wedding ring and his friends' testimonies, police arrested me."

Elias unwrapped a banana that wouldn't last him an hour calorically considering his size and muscle. "How'd you find out he was still alive?"

"One of the friends he'd asked to perjure himself had a change of heart." It was the first domino to fall in a long line of lies unraveled over several months. Months wasted in a prison cell that she'd never get back. "He came forward and gave up my ex's plan. Texts and voicemails he'd kept just in case. After some dealing with the DA's office, he gave up my ex's location. My darling husband had paid for a death certificate, bought a new identity, became someone else—all while I rotted away behind bars. I was released after eight months."

"I'm sorry. I can't begin to imagine what you've been through." Those dark eyes pinned her in place. Held her up with invisible arms like nothing else had since her release. "But I give you my word, I will not fake my death and frame you for my murder as long as we're partners."

Maybe Elias Broyles wasn't so bad for an FBI agent, after all.

"That would be greatly appreciated." Spatters of rain hit the brim of her hat, and she turned her face up to the sky. The cloud had taken over the thin sliver of blue in the past few minutes, and her stomach lurched. The chances of surviving—outrunning—another flash flood were slim. They had to go back. "Another storm is moving in. Come on. We have to get out of here."

Sayles didn't wait for his response as she headed downstream. Back toward that sliver of rock they'd taken solace on last night. There was no telling if it would be enough, but there was no flash flood escape in this corridor. They would die if they pushed through.

"What are you doing? Our killer is this way." Elias pointed upstream. "He's close, Sayles. The bag he dropped is proof. We can catch him. We can stop him."

"Not if we're dead." The rain picked up, stinging her face as the winds barreled down the canyon as though in warning. She studied the rapids. Waited for the debris and the mud and the roar she couldn't forget. "There's nowhere to run—"

A loud boom filled her head.

Elias's mountainous body collided with hers.

Dragging her beneath the river's surface.

Chapter Twelve

He slammed into Sayles.

Elias caught the slight exhale of air crushed from her chest a split second before the river consumed them with cold, watery teeth as sharp as knives. Using his full weight against her, he held them beneath its surface.

Sayles dragged her nails down his arms, over his face. Drawing blood. Fighting against his hold. Fighting for her life. Her kicks missed their targets and failed to dissuade his hold around her.

Someone had shot at them.

Pressure built in his chest as oxygen burned out of his system. He couldn't give the shooter a second chance of hitting his mark, but they wouldn't last long in the river, either. He had to make a choice.

Elias fisted her uniform collar and hauled her above the surface. Water dripped into his eyes, compromised his vision. Her gasp infiltrated his concentration a split second before strong hands shoved against his chest.

Sayles's hat was gone. Lost to the river. She didn't seem to notice as he hauled her behind his back, corralling her into the branching slot canyon they'd stopped in a minute before, his front to hers. Dark hair streaked down her face in rivulets of water. "Get off me—"

"Someone just shot at us." He pressed his hand against her mouth. Pain sliced through the numbness brought on by their swim. Despite the frigid temperatures of the river, her warmth seeped past his soaked clothing and gear. His heart thundered hard, loud enough to drown out the clapping of the waterfall at her back and the roar of the river at his. They were at a disadvantage here. He couldn't hear a damn thing as thunder rumbled overhead. The slot canyon they'd taken shelter in seemed to vibrate along with the storm. Rain only added to his distress. Could they survive another flash flood? Did they have a choice? His training clicked into place, and he ran through their options. None of them great. "Where does this waterfall trail lead?"

"West for about three-quarters of a mile, but it's a dead end and difficult to navigate in places." She shook her head. "There's no way you'd be able to fit through the slots, even if you took off your gear."

They were cornered. Damn it. Elias risked getting a visual of the shooter, but where he'd caught movement on a ledge above the river a few minutes ago, there was nothing but a flash of lightning. The killer was on the move. Aware he wasn't alone. They'd lost the element of surprise, and Elias wouldn't risk Sayles's life to get it back. He spun her around, shoving her down that too-small branch off the main trail. Water kicked up as she stumbled forward. "Then that's where we hide."

"No, it's not." She turned back into him. "The Narrows feeds this slot canyon, and there's no drainage at the end of this branch. If we're on it much longer, it'll flood with no way for us to escape. We have to go back to the main trail. We have to go back downstream."

Where the water had barely crested his ankles while

they'd taken a break, it'd climbed to the middle of his shins. One of the first signs of danger. Soon that roar would fill his head, and they'd be right back where they didn't want to be. In the middle of a flash flood. Except this time, they might not make it out alive. "How long does it take for this branch to flood?"

Elias unholstered his weapon from the small of his back.

"You can't be serious." Sayles shifted her weight between her feet, swiping hair out of her face as the rains intensified. They were protected from the gusts whistling down the canyon, but there was no escaping what came next.

"When did I give you the impression I don't take my job seriously?" Disengaging the magazine, he counted the number of bullets in his weapon, then slammed it back into place with the butt of his palm. "How long, Sayles?"

"If a flood hits, five, maybe ten minutes," she said. "But I've never been dumb enough to test that theory for myself."

"Well, today you get to find out the answer. Let's go." He secured his hand in hers, pulling her past the waterfall and deeper into the unknown. Smooth rock scraped against his shoulders within the first twenty feet as they navigated over rock and gravel-size obstacles. Debris laced the edges of the canyon and added to the suffocation factor.

"This is a mistake." Pulling her hand from his, she surged ahead to take the lead. Always on alert. Always in control. It was what he'd asked of her, and if they were going to make it out of this alive, it would be because of her. "We tell hikers to avoid this section of the trail for a reason."

Elias checked over his shoulder, weapon in hand as

they retreated. As much as he wanted to charge back onto the main trail to confront the son of a bitch who'd taken a shot at them, he wasn't going to lose another innocent life. Never again. "Would you rather get shot?"

He imagined it took everything she had not to respond with whatever retort she'd come up with. Now wasn't the time. They had to move as a team, make decisions as a team. Partners in the purest sense.

Ripples of rock—so much like cresting waves—jutted out and scratched at his arm as he passed. The scratches Sayles had inflicted in the river hadn't broken skin, but he couldn't ignore the sting as adrenaline drained, either. He couldn't blame her in her panic. And, hell, it wasn't the only way she'd left her mark on him these past days. The walls closed in on them, leaving no more than two feet to pass through. Water surged from the direction of the main trail at their back, climbing up his pant legs.

"It's starting. This canyon is going to flood. We need to hurry." Sayles picked up the pace, charging at a blockade of smooth stone that looked as though it'd been set directly in their path. They'd have to climb over to keep going. "Come on."

A second bullet sprayed dust and chunks of rock into Elias's face. Mere inches away.

"Watch out!" He launched forward, using his body to shield Sayles as much as possible. Pain ignited along his arm as fractures of rock rained down from above. Elias spun. And caught the dark shape using the canyon as cover. He pulled the trigger. Enough times to ensure she had a lead. "Go, go, go!"

He couldn't tell if she'd followed his order but trusted Sayles to take care of herself. His pack snagged between the two walls as he retreated backward toward that rock obstacle blocking their path. Elias tried to push through, but his upper body refused to fit.

Then he heard it. The roar.

Water bubbled and turned white as it assaulted the thin slot canyon as violently as a pack of wolves closing in on their prey. He'd lost sight of the killer.

"Elias, take my hand!" Sayles's warning barely registered over the thud of his heartbeat thundering in his ears.

The shooter had disappeared, presumably to find higher ground, but had robbed him and Sayles of their escape. He couldn't fit through the slot, just as she had warned. His pack had caught on one of the rocks. Elias grabbed on to her, his grip slipping through hers. Once. Twice. She climbed back down. Giving up her own escape. In an instant, she'd sliced through the straps of his pack with one of those multi-tools and pulled him through the gap. Her hand was in his before she maneuvered him ahead. Water lapped at their heels, rising faster than he expected. It was different here than on the main trail where the flood could spread out. "Move it!"

They had mere minutes before this canyon was underwater. They'd be lucky if they managed to escape at all, and noting fresh water lines ten, even fifteen feet up the red rock walls, he wasn't sure the chances were good.

Cold seeped around his feet as he climbed higher. They couldn't keep up this pace. His lungs were on fire, his heart ready to beat straight out of his chest. But Sayles remained a constant presence at his back. A comfort in the storm. He reached the top of the incline, ready to sink to his knees in relief.

Sayles's boots slipped against wet stone. Over and over.

The water level was catching up. Going to take her from him. Her eyes widened in realization, and unfiltered fear iced out the confidence he'd become accustomed to over the past two days. Rain plastered her hair against her face, her uniform clinging to her frame. She couldn't get a good grip.

"I've got you." He grabbed for the nearest handhold in the rock with one hand and stretched for her. They weren't going to die today. He wasn't going to lose another innocent life. A foot separated their hands with no way to make up for the difference. "You can do it. Just a little farther."

Her hand trembled as she reached up the ninety-degree incline toward him above. They were going to make it. They had to make it. He couldn't do this without her. The muscles in his jaw ached under the pressure of his teeth. Water climbed to her waist, sucking her into its icy depths, robbing her of any leverage. The rock walls seemed to close in, squeezing the air from his chest as he tried to face her fully. It was impossible with the limited space. Acceptance smoothed fear from her expression. She lowered her hand a fraction of an inch.

And everything in Elias went cold. He shook his head. "Don't you dare. Don't you dare give up. Grab my hand."

"I can't." Weathered red rock betrayed one of the very rangers fighting day in and day out to protect it. River water infiltrated her mouth as she clawed to keep her head above water. Her pack. Her pack would drag her down.

"Come on! You didn't give up on proving you didn't kill your ex. Don't give up now, damn it." Pain flared through his shoulders as he forced his body into the unnatural position on his stomach. Rock bit into his ribs, but he pushed it aside. It didn't matter. He just needed to close that distance between them. It wasn't going to end like this. Not after everything they'd already survived. Not after what she'd been through. This park had become a safe haven when she'd needed it the most. He wouldn't let it kill her. "Now, reach for me!"

Rain splattered against her face as she tried one more time. Her fingertips slipped against his. A last bite of warmth shot through his system. Her boots couldn't get the right angle against the stone. Water churned around her—angry and chaotic—as the river started draining back onto the main trail. Taking her farther from him. Sayles slapped her hands out to grab on to something, anything, to fight against that tide. But it was no use. The walls were too weathered and smooth from centuries of storms just like this one. That foot between them turned into two. Three. The storm hadn't let up. She would die if she got sucked beneath the surface again. "Elias!"

He didn't know what to do. That sour rise of helplessness burned in his throat. Elias abandoned his pack and gauged the drop. Mud and debris made it impossible to measure the depth of the river. He couldn't risk diving. He'd have to jump straight in, and he inhaled a deep breath. His boots took the brunt of the impact as he hit the water's surface. The river swallowed him whole, and it took everything he had to get free of the crushing current working to keep him under. Tumbling end over end. "Sayles!"

No answer. She was already gone.

Chapter Thirteen

Her head throbbed as though her sinuses were infected.

Pressure built in her face, down the back of her neck. Behind her eyes.

Sayles couldn't help the groan of pain as she turned her neck to the side. Liquid drained down the back of her throat, and she turned to cough it up. Something sharp bit into her palms as her stomach heaved.

"Oh, good. You're alive." Footsteps skidded to a halt close by, but it was hard to tell with the cast of shadows. "I wasn't so sure there for a while."

That voice. She didn't recognize it. It seemed to echo, surround her, suffocate her. Jutted rock pressed into her hands as she got her bearings. Alive. She was alive. And wet. "Where am I?"

"Thought you ranger types knew every inch of this park?" His laugh wasn't anything like the warmth she'd wrapped herself in from Elias's. "Guess that saying is true. You learn something new every day."

The park. She was still in Zion. In a...cave? Dark walls had been stained black with minerals and drainage, curving up and over her head. It wasn't a cave per se. Didn't go deep enough, with an oversize opening. An outcropping in the rock. Her heart beat too hard behind her ears to pick up signs of the river. She worked to come up with an answer of how the hell that was possible. She did know every inch of this park, and the last thing she remembered... Cold. Falling. Fear.

Her senses adjusted enough to outline the man in front of her. The one sitting on a flat rock, knees hiked a bit higher, with a spoon in one hand and a bowl of something in the other. A backpack—similar to hers—rested against his thigh. Wait. That *was* her pack.

"Hungry? It's not great straight out of the can, but there's still some left." His features remained in shadow as clouds continued their rampage across the sky through the opening. Rain pummeled and slapped against wet rock a few feet away, tricking her brain into thinking the threat had passed.

The park had been cleared of visitors once word got out there was a killer on the loose. Which meant... Sayles shoved to sit, putting as much distance between them as the outcropping allowed. Her shoulders hit solid wall within a couple of feet. "You."

He offered her a spoonful of whatever he'd been eating, and her stomach rolled with ingested river water. "You look like you could use this more than I do."

She couldn't keep herself together any longer. Curling to one side, she let her stomach have its moment. Water and the small bit of food she'd eaten after waking this morning charged free of her mouth. The small hit of adrenaline dissipated as memories assaulted over and over. Elias. She scanned the half cave. The last image of him—reaching for her from above—intensified the trembling quaking through her. She locked her hands into fists to try to control it, but there was no fighting nature.

Her throat burned as she swallowed around bile and river water. "What...happened?"

"You almost died." The killer set his meal aside, brushing both hands together as though discarding a thick layer of dirt. "I saved you."

That didn't make sense. Sayles searched the half-cave-like structure. For what, she had no idea. An escape. A sign of Elias. A general location of where she'd ended up. Her teeth chattered. The thin cotton uniform she'd worn these past few months only managed to hold on to the chill that refused to leave. "Why?"

Her captor—the killer Elias had been searching the interstate for—shoved to stand. He towered over her. Massive. Intimidating. The kind of man who was fully aware of his size and used it as a weapon against anyone in his way. Probably the same way he'd used it against those motorists he'd murdered. He closed the distance between them, crouching in front of her. Shadows blurred his features, but she could make out a pair of extremely arched eyes. Beard growth aged his face and accentuated the puffy skin beneath those eyes. He wasn't lean. Not in the way Elias had honed layer upon layer of muscle through training and hard work, but the bulk was there. Less defined but just as deadly. Short hair curled over his forehead. Almost boyish apart from the predatory smile splitting his mouth. "You're going to help me."

"I'm not available." Rock cut into her scalp as she tried—and failed—to add just a few more inches of space between them. Reminded all too easily of the way her ex had used his size and strength to get her to comply. But she wasn't that woman anymore. She'd survived his manipulations. And she'd survive this man, too. "Ever."

"But you were all too willing to assist Agent Broyles." He set his arms against his knees. Blocking her escape. Ready to strike at a moment's notice. "Isn't that why you're out here, Ranger Green? To help the FBI catch me."

The shock of her name on his lips must've registered on her face before she had a chance to shut it down. Her name tag. She closed her eyes against the stupidity of that realization. Of course he knew her name. She was still wearing her name tag. Sayles tried to swallow down the uncertainty in her voice. "I go where I'm told."

"That's good." An unnatural stillness seized the killer in front of her. "Because right now I need you to get me out of this park without the police or your agent following. Understand?"

She shook her head as best she could, every cell in her body focused on the wide opening at his back. No recognition of their surroundings, but she hadn't been unconscious that long. Right? He had to have brought her somewhere off the Narrows trail, which meant she could find Elias. They could stop this killer from hurting anyone else. "I can't do that."

"Of course you can." He stood, once again towering over her, using his size to force her compliance. "Otherwise, I have no need for you."

She locked her gaze on his face. Trying to memorize every detail, every scar, or tattoo or identifying characteristic. In case she got out of this alive. "Are you going to kill me?"

"Only if I have to." He shrugged as if the idea of murder was nothing more than a passing inconvenience.

"You make it sound like I have a choice." Despite her two-day trek in the middle of a river, her mouth had gone dry. She gauged her chances of running for the entrance and getting a head start before he caught up with her. They weren't looking good from her current position. "Did all your other victims get the same choice or did you make the decision for them?"

Elias would find her. She didn't know how. She didn't know if he'd managed to escape that slot canyon, and she didn't want to think about the possibility he hadn't. But she had to believe in something. The agent she'd agreed to guide through the park yesterday afternoon wasn't the man she'd come to know in the hours since. He was better. Understanding. Protective. The kind of man who believed evil should never go unpunished. So unlike the other federal agents she'd known throughout her life and her marriage. No matter what happened, she knew Elias would fight for her.

"Someone's been talking about me." That smile was back. Slick and oily with a hint of violence. "Tell me, Ranger Green, if you agree to get me out of this park unnoticed, will you share a tent with me, too?"

Nausea charged through her. He'd been watching them. Studying them. How close had he gotten without them noticing? She and Elias had assumed he'd been ahead of them on the trail, but what if he'd just been biding his time? A small piece of the courage it'd taken to stand up to her ex electrified her nerves. She raised her chin. She wouldn't cower. She wouldn't beg. If anything that would give this man exactly what he wanted—what her ex had wanted—and she'd grown tired of making herself smaller for other's comfort. "Sure. As long as you're not scared I'll kill you in your sleep."

His laugh rippled through her, raising warning in its

wake. He crouched in front of her again, consuming her focus. Then gripped her chin harder than necessary to force her attention. "Hold on to that fight. You're going to need it."

Sayles ripped from his grasp and managed to summon enough saliva to spit at his face. Stars exploded as his hand connected to her jaw. Her body hit the unforgiving cave floor against her will. Pain unlike anything she'd experienced cocooned her in a never-ending echo. Tears sprang to her eyes. She couldn't fight them. Couldn't swallow the sob escaping her chest. Of all the manipulation, the abuse and the danger she'd survived, a single strike was the catalyst that would unravel her. She held her face as she righted herself, breaking off a piece of rock about as big as her hand.

"We leave in ten minutes. I suggest you eat something and get some fluids in you." The killer retraced his steps back to that rock she'd found him on upon waking and tossed her backpack at her. The bag landed at her feet, supplies shifting out of order. He'd gone through it. Most likely took her multi-tool to keep her from attacking him. "We're not stopping until you get me out of this hellhole."

She closed her hand around the sharpened rock. From the looks of the cave, he'd gone out of his way to ensure there wouldn't be anything she could use against him. But he hadn't planned for her fall to break off a chunk. Rangers fought against damaging the park's natural features, but she couldn't miss this opportunity, either. Her gaze cut to the entrance. She just needed to buy herself more time. Think this through while keeping her makeshift weapon to herself. "It's still raining. The trail is flooded. It's too dangerous—"

"Then what good are you?" Collecting his own supplies, he slung his pack over his shoulders and stared her down. Daring her to disobey.

Sayles shifted the rock behind her, pinning it between her low back and the cave wall. "You won't get far with a captive in tow. The FBI is going to catch up to you."

"Maybe." Another shrug. "Or maybe I leave your body for him to find. That would slow your agent down, don't you think?"

Elias wasn't hers. She was fairly certain he didn't even like her, which fit her plans to avoid federal agents and men in general as long as she lived. But that lonely part of her—the one who'd always wanted and believed in happily-ever-afters—protested at her decision to isolate herself in the middle of a national park in the name of freedom. And it'd certainly enjoyed waking up plastered against his chest this morning.

"Seven minutes." He set himself against the arched entrance, arms folded across that massive chest. Waiting. "You're wasting time, Ranger Green. I will drag you out of this cave if I have to because I know you can still navigate while bleeding."

"Fine." Did she have any other choice in her current circumstances? He had a point. She wouldn't get far on an empty stomach and dehydration. Hikers had died in this very park with more in their stomachs than she had right now. After rummaging through her supply pack, Sayles discovered he had indeed taken her multi-tool. She extracted a bag of dried protein oatmeal and downed it as fast as she could, following it up with a couple swigs of water. Carefully repacking her bag with one hand, she shifted the severed rock into her pack without notice. And left something else behind. Elias had no idea what kind of monster they were hunting. This was her chance to find out. Sayles pushed herself to her feet and slung her drenched pack into place. "Let's go."

Chapter Fourteen

She was gone.

Elias blinked up into that dark, raging sky. Cliffs angled into his vision. Hell. His body ached. He couldn't feel his toes or fingers. Something was digging into his back. Rain pattered against his face as he raised his upper body off the ground. The river receded from the slot canyon a few feet away, its icy fingers trying to take him with it. Water sprayed into his face from above. That waterfall. The one they'd stopped under before the killer had tried to shoot them. At least he knew where he'd ended up.

He remembered jumping in after Sayles. And then... Nothing. He should've been swept downstream with her. Maybe if he'd spent the past few months in the gym instead of stalking convenience stores along the interstate for signs of their killer—and, let's be honest, road snacks—he might've been. Thank heaven for the extra few pounds he'd gained on this case.

"Damn it." Pain seared through his rib cage as he twisted. Blood. Debris. Elias sucked in a deep breath as he pulled at the stained edges of his shirt to get a better view. A twig, no more than six inches in length and about as round as his little finger, had embedded itself between two ribs. Thankfully not deep enough to deflate a lung. He set himself back down. Thought about what to do next.

Sayles was out here. Because of him. Because of his insistence of taking this trail to escape the shooter. It'd been a bad call that might cost the ranger her life.

He'd abandoned his pack in the slot canyon. The winding maze of rock and smooth lines kept him from spotting it from here, but he couldn't risk going back onto the main trail without it. Lifting his head again, he pinched the middle of the twig. And pulled.

Agony ripped through his torso. His scream bounced off the surrounding rock and shot it straight into the clouds above. Staring at the wound, he counted off the seconds. Waiting. It didn't seem to be—

Blood bubbled to fill the hole the twig had left behind, and he clamped a hand to apply pressure. Little humor coated the laugh rocking through him. "Well, now you're going to bleed to death. Great work, Broyles."

Damn it. He needed Sayles. Her know-how, her first aid kit. Elias hauled himself to his feet, stumbling as a rush of dizziness attacked. Pea-size rocks shifted beneath his feet. He spotted thousands of them between him and his pack now that the slot canyon had drained, each one working to slow him down. One hand pressed into his side, he followed the winding path to the area where he'd dropped his pack.

Memories of Sayles's scream, his name tearing from her throat, as she tried to reach for his hand threatened to convince him to turn around. Forget about the pack. Go after her. But he wouldn't make it far without addressing his wound. He needed that pack. Setting his foot against a blocklike section of stone, Elias tried to climb one-handed.

Wouldn't work. The angles and the slick surface of rock worked against him, but taking pressure off his wound guaranteed he'd bleed out that much faster.

There was no other way.

The section of the trail where he'd left his pack was at least eight feet above. He'd have to two-hand it and pray the damn thing hadn't been washed away. He could do this. He had to do this. For Sayles. He wasn't going to lose another life on his watch. He'd promised to keep her alive. To make up for the past by protecting her through-out this manhunt. Nothing would stop him from finding her. Focused on how he'd get up the incline, he took short breaths, hyping himself up. "Come on."

He released the pressure on his wound. Blood instantly swarmed to the surface and spread through the soaked ma-terial of his shirt. Ignoring the bleeding, he shoved off the foothold and stretched one hand overhead, locking onto a handhold above. His other hand braced against the wall to his left. Now he just had to climb. The pain swelled. His heart rate skyrocketed. Warm liquid pooled along the waistband of his pants with every inch he climbed.

Seconds stretched into minutes. Minutes into an hour. His fingers ached as he tightened his hold against slick rock determined to buck him free. Finally, Elias threw himself over the lip of the incline, sprawling out across the cold stone with nothing left to give. And faced a min-iature cliff off the other side. The world threatened to tear out from under him as he caught himself from going over the twenty-foot-plus drop.

His pack dug into his shoulder. Luck. Pure luck he hadn't kicked it over. Dragging himself back from the edge, he focused on stopping the leak from his side. Elias extracted his first aid kit and popped the lid. His vision wavered as he pressed his hand deeper into the wound. What had Sayles said about these waters being infested? Something about water toxins. He had to clean the wound first. Make sure it didn't get infected. That was what she'd done on his thigh. All right. He'd have to use his drinking water.

"Clean the wound." He could do that. Lifting his shirt, he pressed the hem beneath his chin to pinch it against his chest. Brown bits of dirt and crusted blood clung to the edges. He unscrewed the top to his water bottle and irrigated the hole as best as he could. The angle didn't give him complete visibility to ensure everything had been cleaned out, but it would have to work for now. Time was running out. No burn this time. He wasn't sure if that was a good thing or not. He used the gauze pads in the kit to dry around the twig hole, sprayed the blood-clotting spray and replaced the old gauze with a new layer before taping it down. "Okay. You might not die today."

He couldn't say the same for his partner.

Repacking everything as quickly as he could, Elias dragged his pack after him since Sayles had cut the straps in order to save his life. He descended the drop. The pain in his rib cage downgraded from a throb to an annoyance, but there was no telling if he'd done any of it right to avoid infection. He retraced his steps toward the main trail.

The river hadn't finished throwing its temper tantrum. Water levels were still much too high to navigate it safely, but the time for hesitation had passed. He had to find Sayles. Had to avoid getting shot, too. He patted the holster at his back. Hell. His gun. Scanning the area in tight circles, he couldn't see where the weapon had gone.

Which created a whole lot of problems in and of itself. He couldn't risk hunting the Hitchhiker Killer without some form of protection or having some kid find a gun along a very public and popular trail when the park reopened. "Now's not the time."

Elias dove straight back into the river's grip, taking it downstream. Sayles had known. She'd told him the risks of getting caught in the slot canyon during a flash flood, and he hadn't listened. Now she was the one paying the price. That pressure kept him moving. Kept him angry. "Sayles!"

No sign of her natural-colored uniform or pack. No body caught on one of the many logs stretching across the trail or rocks. The current forced him to pick up his pace when his body wanted nothing more than to rest after being thrown around as much as he had been on this trail. One thing was for sure. Once he caught the killer, he'd never hike this trail again.

Sayles was smart. She knew this trail better than anyone. If there was a chance of survival, she would've taken it by getting to higher ground. He scanned the domineering cliffs watching over him and anyone else who came through this insane maze. From this position, there was no telling whether he could climb higher. Everything looked too smooth. He'd try farther downstream and hike back if needed, but his gut told him she'd gotten out. That she'd saved herself.

"I'm coming." He wasn't sure who he was trying to convince more, Sayles or himself, that he wasn't going to stand by and fight this alone. That he wasn't going to fail her like he'd failed the witness in his last investigation. Exhaustion slowed him down, but he wouldn't let it get the best of him. His partner needed him, and he'd be there for her the same way he'd be there for Grant if he were in this situation.

Water had long infiltrated his gear and pooled in his boots. He didn't want to imagine the blisters he'd leave this canyon with, but he was sure Sayles would help him with those as she'd helped him before. That was the kind of woman she was. She'd guarded that heart of hers against any threat thanks to her ex, but there were still pieces that couldn't be killed off. And for the first time since that disaster of a date two years ago, Elias found himself wanting one of those pieces. Wanting more of her smile. More of her determination and courage and intensity in his life. The backtalk and teasing and biting comments. He wanted it all. She'd lit something in him that'd been buried in him. Made him feel alive. He wasn't ready to give that up.

Every muscle in his legs protested the downstream descent, but he caught sight of a thin edge of rock that seemed to lead higher up the cliff face on the opposite side of the trail. If Sayles had escaped the flash flood, it seemed the perfect spot to gain the advantage until the storm died down. Rain kept pummeling down on top of him, weighing him down and increasing the risk of crossing, but there really wasn't any other choice. Not when it came to Sayles. He'd dragged her into this mess. He would be the one to get her out.

Elias charged through the raging currents, avoiding whitecaps and sticking to the boulders still peeking above the surface. It took longer than he wanted with the injury in his side, but within a few minutes, he'd reached the opposite riverbank. The edge of rock climbing overhead was nothing more than a thin, graveled trail rangers had likely advised hikers to avoid, but he'd take the chance. To find her.

His thighs screamed for relief as he ascended the incline, one foot after the other, until he'd reached a flatter section ending in nothing more than a half cave that provided little to no protection against the onslaught of rain and wind. Except there was something…functional about the small cavern. A flat rock took up residence in the center with fine grain sand kicked up around it. As if someone had indeed used this undersize barricade to escape the floods of the past two days. Heavier drops of water collected along the arched entrance and tapped against his shoulders and scalp as he moved inside. He barely managed to stand at his full height. Could stretch his arms out straight and brush both walls with his fingertips.

Someone had been here.

The footprints in the sand had gone undisturbed. And there. Against the wall. Elias crouched to a spread of tracks, picking up a tube of antibiotic ointment. The same brand she'd used to tend his thigh wound yesterday. Sayles. She'd been here. Right here. Had left this tube as a message, knowing he wouldn't stop the search, which meant she hadn't been alone.

He pocketed the ointment and turned to face the arched entrance. They had to be close. On the move. Stepping out into the storm, Elias hiked higher. "I'm coming for you, partner."

Chapter Fifteen

She was going to die.

Sayles fought to keep her balance as they hiked 2,000 feet above the Narrows on a goat trail no more than two feet in width. Park visitors and rangers alike were warned against setting foot on this path. With no handholds and the potential for falling rocks, no one had wanted to take the risk. Until now. A nudge from behind tightened the muscles in her jaw and neck. "Unless you want to take a dive headfirst off this trail, stop crowding me."

"Come on now, Ranger Green." Another brush of his hand against her waist. Purposeful. Meant to show domination. Show her who was in charge, even out here. "You and I have the same goal. To escape. That should make us friends."

"You don't know anything about me." The added weight to her pack threatened to pitch her backward into his frame. The rock she'd hidden wasn't much, but it might be the difference between escape or ending up dead whenever the bastard was done using her.

"Well, that's just not true." His voice took on a more distant tone, not quite directed at her. Like he was scanning their surroundings. She didn't dare to look back to confirm one way or another. "I know your name is Sayles. That you've been a ranger here in Zion for the past five months. Came all the way from Colorado, didn't you? Alone. With an art history degree of all things. Not a whole lot of work in that arena, but that's not why you ended up in one of the most isolated national parks in the west. Something must've scared you. Made you run from your hometown."

The ache in her jaw intensified. She wasn't going to give him the details. Wasn't going to give him anything other than a reason to regret forcing her help. "You read my résumé. Congratulations. You're officially a detective."

That oily laugh dredged through her and turned her stomach.

"Why try to escape through the park? It's all just wilderness at the end of this trail. There's nowhere for you to run." Gravel shifted under her weight. The storm hadn't let up, turning solid ground into inches of wet sand. She had to watch her footing. One wrong step and she'd end up a park statistic.

"That's not really any of your concern, is it?" He kept pace with her better than she expected, dashing her hopes of gaining distance in order to run. "Getting me through the park without being noticed by the backcountry patrols. That's what you should be focusing on."

It was getting harder to breathe at this elevation. The oatmeal she'd eaten dry was beginning to turn in her stomach. Her heart rate had risen into fleeting, shallow pulses. Every step higher brought on the risk of altitude sickness despite Zion's 4,000-foot dominance above sea level and her acclimation over these past few months. Turning her head slightly, she kept the killer at her back within sight. Searching for those telltale signs of slowing down, vomiting, dizziness. If she caught him off guard, she might be able to survive. "That hiker you killed at the bottom of the trail. Why him?"

"You're mighty curious, Ranger Green." He studied her as a scientist studied a bug he didn't like. "Could it be you're trying to pump me for information to hand over to the FBI in hopes of making it out of this alive?"

She locked down the shudder taking her by surprise. Sayles wouldn't let him see the effect of that thought. Of dying within the very park that'd gifted her a new life. One of freedom and choice. "If you plan on killing me once we get to the end of the trail, what's the harm of unburdening yourself along the way?"

"You think I feel guilty for killing those people?" Not with that smile she didn't. "You'd be barking up the wrong tree."

"So all of this is just some sick game to you?" Scanning the trail ahead, she tried to come to terms with her situation. Of being alone 2,000 feet up on a too-narrow trail with a man who could end her right here if the thought crossed his mind. She hadn't fought for this new life to end up dead now. Not without going out on her own terms. "You'll kill anyone who gets in your way without so much as thinking it through?"

"All I've been doing is thinking this through." The words were nothing more than a whisper nearly lost to the winds. Something maybe she wasn't supposed to hear.

Sayles didn't know what to say to that, what to think. It didn't matter. She'd never hiked this trail, wasn't sure where it led or if there was an end. For all she knew, she could be leading them straight over the edge of a cliff. Goats could jump up cliff faces. Humans not so much.

Either way, she was running out of time before her usefulness was all used up. She had to act. To give Elias and his partner something if this ended poorly. She owed him that after he'd saved her life yesterday. "Do you at least have a name? Or should I just call you the Hitchhiker Killer?"

"It's got a certain ring to it, doesn't it?" He cocked his head as a predator might when confronted with prey. "But if that's too much of a mouthful for you, you can call me Patrick."

"Not your real name, I'm guessing." The trail crested the top of the north cliff overlooking the Narrows. She could see the river below, identify the curve leading into Wall Street Corridor. Most hikers turned around at this point where the river split into an upstream branch leading east into Orderville Canyon. Park visitors were prohibited from heading that way due to the canyon walls becoming so narrow they were virtually impassable and the clay soil making the trek too slippery. They were close to that junction. Right where she'd intended to lead Elias to set up camp before they'd had to stop to treat her hypothermia symptoms. Even now, that base chill refused to let up, and she wanted nothing more than to fall asleep beside Elias's heat. To inhale his earthy and masculine scent that clung to her hair and skin where she'd touched him.

"You'd be right." The killer didn't offer anything more.

Sayles caught the slight change in his step. A little too close to the edge. She'd picked up her pace, forcing him to keep up, to ascend several hundred feet too fast. Depending on his elevation experience, acute mountain sickness could set in as quickly as a few minutes. This was her shot. The one chance to get away. The goat trail they'd commandeered became even thinner ahead with a slight decline on the other side. She didn't want to be here. Didn't want Patrick—or whatever the hell his name was—to reach the end of the trail. Because who knew if the FBI would be able to catch up? Who knew how many more people would get hurt or killed if she helped him reach Big Spring? The lie slipped from her mouth with that in mind. "I need to stop. I'm getting lightheaded."

She didn't wait for an answer, pressing her back against the rock wall. Dark clouds kissed the peaks above, and that chill she couldn't get rid of only worsened as crystalized air brushed over the exposed skin of her face and neck. It was only then she realized she'd lost her hat to the river below. Risner would definitely be taking it out of her next paycheck, but she'd stomach the cost if it meant getting out of this alive.

"Fine." Patrick swung his pack to his front, his eyes a little more glazed than she remembered from the outcropping she'd woken up inside. Not as hard. "Two minutes, and don't even think about trying to run for it. I will catch you, and I will make you pay for trying."

"I wouldn't dream of it." She'd expected an argument, which meant he'd been experiencing lightheadedness and didn't want to admit he might not have been as prepared for this escape as he wanted to let on. One shot. That was all she had. Sayles maneuvered her own pack front-side and drove her hand inside. Around the rock she'd stashed at the bottom. She didn't know how to do this. Hurt someone. The inclination had come so easily to her ex. "It's called acute mountain sickness."

Patrick took a second too long to divert his attention from the opposite cliff face to her. "What?"

"That thing you're feeling right now." She gripped

the rock tighter, still hidden by her pack. "The sluggish-ness, disorientation. Your brain isn't getting enough oxy-gen at these elevations. You've probably had a headache since yesterday, but the longer you're here, the worse your symptoms will get."

"I know what altitude sickness is." A hint of breath-lessness softened his bite. "Start walking."

"Sure. But climbing higher isn't going to help you. At this point, nothing will." Sayles extracted the rock, sure to keep it hidden as she reset her pack on her back.

Then swung.

The impact of rock against skull reverberated through her hand. It hurt. A lot. The shock waves forced her to drop the weapon entirely. His groan punctured through the too-fast thud of her heart between her ears. She spun, launching herself ahead. Not looking back. She couldn't get enough air. While she'd acclimated to the park, adren-aline flooded her veins and took control.

"You b—" His rage seared down her back. Too close. Too close. The pounding of boots closed in.

Muscles she'd only recently developed protecting this park locked up at the sudden demand of exertion. A cramp skewed her calf as the trail dipped lower, and she nearly face-planted from the change in angle. Mud suctioned to her boots, providing a clear path straight to her. No matter where she went, he would find her. He would catch her. He would kill her. Faster. She had to run faster, but the unfa-miliarity of the trail demanded caution she couldn't afford to spare. Aches screamed for attention. Her breathing too shallow. Black edged into her vision. No. She wasn't going to pass out. Not yet. Sayles searched for somewhere—

anywhere—she could hide. To get her bearings. To gauge how close he'd gotten.

A quick check over her shoulder confirmed she'd added some distance between them. But was it enough? She turned face forward.

And caught sight of the sheer end of the goat trail.

Momentum threatened to throw her over the edge. Pulling back, she threw her hands out to grab on to anything that might keep her from going over. Her fingertips met nothing but smooth rock face, but she'd stopped just in time.

Giving Patrick a chance to catch up. She had to keep moving. Hide.

Except there was nowhere to go. Out of breath, Sayles gauged the distance between her side of the goat trail across the cavern of emptiness to the other. The rains surged down the slope between the two halves of the trail. Could she make it? Would the soggy ground support her weight? She didn't have a choice, did she? Not unless she wanted to end up as another notch in the Hitchhiker Killer's belt.

She backed up a couple feet. Determination similar to that she'd relied on to escape her ex surged. Shifting her weight into her toes, Sayles charged forward.

Searing pain rippled across her scalp.

Her back hit a wall of muscle, the growl in her ear pooling dread at the base of her spine. "Going somewhere, Ranger Green?"

"Please." She didn't know what she was begging for. He hadn't taken mercy on the five victims he'd slaughtered. Why would her pleas make any difference? She couldn't stop her whimper as desperation and survival won out.

"I warned you what would happen if you ran." Fisting

her hair, he angled her head back into his shoulder. Exposing her throat. The tang of blood burned in her nostrils.

"You're going to want to take your hands off my partner." Elias's mass solidified in her vision, dangerous and formidable. "Right the hell now."

The world shifted as Patrick—the Hitchhiker Killer—swung her around. Using her as a shield.

Elias. He was alive. He'd come for her. The relief was temporary as she took in the bloodstain spread across his torso. His breathlessness.

"Agent Broyles, you made it just in time." Patrick released his hold on her hair.

Just before he shoved her over the cliff.

Chapter Sixteen

Her scream would follow him into his nightmares.

"Sayles!" Elias charged forward, hand outstretched as though there was a damn thing he could do to stop her from falling. Blood drained from his upper body in a rush. Dead. She was dead. Added to the growing list of victims in this bastard's wake. He couldn't breathe, couldn't think straight. How? How had this happened? How had it gone so horribly wrong so quickly?

The man in front of him peered over the edge where the ranger had gone over. Not an accident. Pushed off. Blood rippled down sharp features and caught in the killer's facial hair. A wicked, slithering smile spread the bastard's lips thin. "Well, will you look at that. Ranger Green has claws."

What?

Breath crushed from his chest as he caught movement at the end of the thin trail he'd followed her on. A boot swung into view, and the world stopped turning. She'd caught herself. Saved herself. Dangling 2,000 feet above the earth. One slip. That was all it would take to lose her, and Elias wasn't sure he could take it.

"Sayles." He took that step. The one that would get him closer to pulling her to safety. But was stopped by the killer standing between them. Elias's fingers tingled for the weight of his weapon lost to the river below, and he dropped his pack off to the side. Fisting his hands, he reminded himself of why he was here. To stop a killer. To keep the son of a bitch from escaping custody.

"I'm sorry, Agent Broyles. Did you really think it would be so easy?" The Hitchhiker Killer wasn't anything Elias had expected. Though the crazed look in his eye certainly fit the bill of a serial killer. The attacker cracked his neck to one side, taking his own step forward. "You've been hunting me these past few weeks. You had to have known I would've prepared for this, and I can't very well have you following me to my final destination."

Sayles's sob drove through him. The rains wouldn't make it easy to hold on for much longer, but he had to trust her to take care of herself for now as the threat edged closer. "You talk this much to those motorists you gutted, or am I special?"

That smile didn't falter as the killer pulled a gleaming blade from the back of his waistband. "Don't forget that hiker. He got an earful, too."

"You're going to pay for every one of them." Elias braced for the oncoming fight. Battle-ready tension taking over. "I don't care how long it takes me. I will have you in cuffs."

The killer lunged knife-first. His movement worked against him as Elias dodged the attack. The blade slipped along Elias's chest, a mere inch away from cutting through him. He latched on to the killer's wrist and turned the tip of the steel straight into the Hitchhiker Killer's face, shoving the bastard into the cliff, putting his own back to the 2,000-foot drop.

Surprise and something along the lines of humor laced

the killer's expression as Elias struggled to inch that knife closer, but sheer strength fought back. A knee slammed into Elias's gut, and he lost his leverage on the killer's wrist. Pain sparked through his torso thanks to that damn twig that'd impaled between his ribs, and he doubled over to counter the effects. Soggy gravel bit into his knees as he hit the ground. The Hitchhiker Killer stepped free.

"Elias!" Sayles's pleas notched his blood pressure higher and called to something deeper. Had the witness he'd sent to her death begged for him to save her in her last moments? Would he have been able to save her if he'd been there?

"Hang on!" Elias blocked the arc of the blade aimed for his face. Striking as fast as possible, he launched his elbow into the killer's jaw. His attacker's head snapped back. Giving him the few seconds of disorientation he needed to get to Sayles. He jumped for the end of the trail, both hands curling over the edge.

Brazen and unfiltered fear contorted her beautiful face as she whipped her gaze to him. The knuckles of her fingers were white against red rock. She couldn't hang on for much longer. "Help me. Please. Help me."

He wrapped his hands around both of her wrists and pulled with everything he had. It wasn't enough. Memories of them in the same position, of her relying on him to protect her—to save her—from the river clawing through the canyon, had him screaming against the effort straining his injured ribs. He'd failed her then. He wouldn't fail her now. "I've got you. I won't let go."

She put her trust in him, loosening her hold on the rocks she clung to. Her eyes widened a split second later, cutting to something over his shoulder. "Look out!"

Agony ripped across his side, and he lost the grip on one of her wrists. Sayles's weight pulled her down. She swung, her pack skimming against the rock face. Another scream escaped her control as she twisted in his hold, dangling by his grip alone. The killer penetrated his peripheral vision. Elias braced for the second kick, and he nearly lost his hold on his partner altogether. "Reach!"

The order barely left his mouth before Sayles was clawing to regain her grip. Toes digging into the side of the drop-off, she scrambled for purchase, but the rock and mud simply crumbled under her weight. She dropped again. Lower. Water reduced the friction between his hands. He was losing his grip on her, and they both knew it.

A shadow slipped over him. Lightning sparked, solidifying the killer's proximity.

"I think this is one of those 'if I can't have her, no one will' situations, Agent Broyles." Heaving breaths reached his ears as the Hitchhiker Killer carved his blade downward. Directly for Elias's spine.

Sayles locked onto a rock and pulled her wrist from his hands. "Move!"

He rolled into the cliff face, putting solid rock at his back. He was at a disadvantage as steel cut across his face and imbedded into the shifting gravel above his shoulder. Stinging pain spread across his cheek, followed by a flood of warmth. Blood. The attacker had come close to sending that blade home. Shoving everything he had into his next attack, Elias kicked out and made contact with the killer's chest.

He didn't give his assailant time to regain his balance and surged to his feet. Catching the Hitchhiker Killer around the waist, Elias hauled the bastard up and back and slammed him into the ground. Except he hadn't accounted for the narrowness of the trail. His knee slipped off the edge, and it was only his hold around the suspect in his arm that kept him from going over completely.

The knife slipped through the small gap between their bodies, and Elias barely managed to avoid its tip sinking into his chest. He bent the killer's wrist at an unnatural angle, forcing the him to release the blade. A scream ripped from the man's throat as the knife plunged toward the Narrows below.

"Elias, I can't hold on!" Sayles needed him to finish this. To get them the hell off this trail.

He rocketed his fist into the Hitchhiker Killer's face. Once. Twice.

"Is that the best you've got, Agent Broyles?" That serpentine smile only spread wider as the bastard's head bounced off pea-size gravel underneath them. Blood dribbled from his mouth, lost to the biting rain slashing through the too-thin air.

Elias hit him again. Knocking the killer unconscious. Something released from around his rib cage, and he crawled off the suspect's body. "Sayles."

Diving for the end of the trail, he grabbed the collar of her uniform shirt. The cotton threatened to tear in his grasp, but it gave him some sense of friction compared to her bare skin. "Hold on to my neck."

The ranger stabbed her toes into the crumbling mountainside and hurled her weight upward. Her arms secured around his neck, and Elias dragged her over the lip. Holding her against him, unwilling or unable to let her go, he didn't know. She was alive. She was real. She was here. "It's okay. I've got you."

Sobs racked her upper body, and Elias held on to her tighter. The lip of the trail disappeared under his heels as he kicked them a few feet back from the edge. Threading his fingers into her hair, he buried his face in to her neck, letting her use him for however long she needed. "He was going to kill me if I didn't get him out of the park."

"I know." Elias framed her face, pulling her back to get a better look. He scanned the length of her body for any signs of blood or injury. "Are you okay? Are you hurt?"

She shook her head. "No. He didn't hurt me, but I can't say the same for him."

"Good." He wasn't sure what came over him, why every cell in his body urged him to close that short distance between them, but he had nothing left in his arsenal to avoid it. Elias crushed his mouth to hers. This beautiful, confident, inspiring woman who a mere twenty-four hours ago couldn't stand being in the same room as him. There was nothing sweet and romantic about the kiss. A frenzy had started the moment he'd realized she'd been taken and hadn't let up. Every second of concern and fear laced each stroke of his mouth against hers until he had to break to catch his breath. Setting his forehead against hers, Elias breathed her in. Tried to convince his nervous system the danger was over. "I'm sorry. I'm sorry I wasn't able to keep him from taking you."

Blood blended with water between her fingers. "It wasn't your fault. I knew you were coming for me." She interlaced her hands with his on either side of her face. "I knew you wouldn't give up."

"Never." Reality tendriled into his awareness. They weren't safe up here. At any moment, the trail could fail altogether, and he'd never forgive himself if something happened to Sayles because he couldn't keep his mouth to himself. "We need to get the hell out of here."

She nodded as if just realizing their situation. Water streaked down her face, and Sayles swiped it away to clear her vision. Most likely missing that iconic hat of hers. "We're above Orderville Canyon Junction. We should be able to camp there until the storm passes."

"Good. Then let's get moving." Elias helped her maneuver off his lap, instantly missing the heat she'd generated. Then the pain moved in. Hell. He'd forgotten about the hole in his side. "I might also need you to patch me up again. Seems I got into a fight with a twig."

Sayles didn't answer. Didn't even seem to breathe.

He followed the direction of her gaze over his shoulder. And froze. "Damn it."

Surging to his feet, he searched for signs of movement. Of something to give them an idea of where the hell the killer had gone. He couldn't have just vanished. Had his unconscious body gone over the trail's edge, or had the Hitchhiker Killer managed to escape without notice? Elias couldn't see the bottom of the canyon clearly from here. Not with the storm attacking from every angle.

"Come on." He grabbed for his pack with one hand and for Sayles's hand with the other. He wasn't letting her out of his sight from here on out and headed along the trail he assumed was meant for pack horses rather than actual human beings. Toward that cave where he'd found her antibiotic ointment.

They'd barely managed to survive between two flash floods, hypothermia, a rogue twig and a killer determined to get away with murder, but one thing was for sure. "This isn't over."

Chapter Seventeen

It took longer to set up the tent than it should have.

Between the gashes on her palms and the wound in Elias's side, they were moving slower than either of them wanted, but the storm had given them a slight reprieve. In the end, neither of them had even bothered pretending to want to sleep in separate tents. They didn't have the energy by the time they'd collapsed onto their sleeping bags or to fight the incessant need for warmth. And connection, in her case.

Sayles stripped free of her wet uniform with sore muscles that fought her at every turn as Elias did the same on the other side of the tent. There really wasn't that much room between them. Her tent had been structured for one person, and she collided with his shoulder or arm more than once as the weight of this assignment pressed in. A single spear of sunlight reached the bottom of the canyon, but seemed to go out of its way to avoid them, and she couldn't fight the responding chill.

They hadn't spoken a word to each other since descending down that too-thin goat trail that'd nearly killed them. Didn't want to acknowledge the fact that the Hitchhiker Killer had gotten away, that he had won, leaving them to do nothing but lick their wounds. Elias had held her hand the entire time, as if he couldn't stand the thought of letting her out of his reach, and she'd been just as desperate. Her awareness of the federal agent prodding at the medical tape from his bare torso only grew through the unending exhaustion trying to drag her down. He'd come for her. Risked his life for her. Saved her. "Thank you" didn't feel like enough.

Elias flinched against some invisible pain as he lifted the tape and gauze to get a better view of his wound.

"Here. Let me." Relieved of her soaked uniform, she realized she should've been embarrassed about the fact there was nothing between them other than the thin material of her oversize T-shirt from her recovered pack. But she couldn't summon the internal argument. Sayles skimmed her fingers around the edge of the dressing, reveling in his instant body heat soothing the scrapes on her hands, and peeled the gauze away to get a better look. He'd done a good job cleaning the small hole. Managed to stop the bleeding. "It doesn't look so bad. What did you clean it with?"

"My drinking water." His voice sounded as though it'd been raked over gravel. From screaming, from tiredness, from debris in the water he'd swallowed. Almost…broken.

The effect chased back that relentless need to keep her mask in place, to be the woman he'd met in the visitors' center. The one who could keep herself together despite their circumstances. Maybe right now she could just…be. Acknowledge that they'd been through something terrible and leave expectations outside the tent. As rewarding as it'd been to disappear in Zion, to start making her own choices and discover who she was without a manipulative bastard calling the shots, wasn't letting go another kind of freedom? "Good choice."

"I learned from the best." The weight of his gaze burned her scalp, but Elias held utterly still as she inspected the wound. It wasn't deadly. However, infection took root in all kinds of circumstances, and they couldn't take the chance. Not with the killer still out there. Potentially watching them as he had these past two days.

Grabbing for her pack, she twisted to pull her first aid kit free and spread the supplies she'd need. "You mean my survival cards."

"No. Not the cards." The whisper contradicted the fierceness with which he'd kissed her on that trail. As though his entire being depended on consuming her from the inside out. He'd done a fantastic job. She could still feel the press of his mouth against hers, the heat they'd shared, the desperation. It'd awoken something in her she hadn't felt for a long time. Not just her physical desire but the desire to feel wanted, to no longer be ignored and small. In those rare seconds, Elias had eradicated her deep need to slide through life unnoticed and alone. He'd empowered her to make the next call. And she wanted more.

"I have more alcohol." Redressing his wound was all she could focus on to keep that crazed want in check. She wasn't sure she'd ever been kissed like that. From the beginning, her ex had made her feel owned, and there'd been a kind of safety that came with it. At first. Instead of choice, he'd taken the brunt of their decisions—her decisions—and convinced her it was for the best. The fewer decisions she had to make, the more energy she had to focus on him, his needs, their relationship. It'd somehow made sense, but over the years that ownership had turned to domination. To belittling and criticizing any attempts to take control of her own life. Questioning her loyalty and commitment to their marriage. A long con. That was what it'd felt like. Like she'd signed up for one thing but had wound up with nothing in the end. Slowly and meticulously destroying everything that made her...her. Shaping her into someone she didn't recognize in the mirror, the damage irreparable.

Sayles dabbed a fresh pad of gauze with alcohol and pressed it against Elias's wound. He sucked in a deep breath through his teeth, and she pulled back. "Sorry. I know it stings, but it'll lower chances of infection."

"I trust you." Elias notched his head back on his shoulders, staring up at the top of the tent.

Her heart shuddered in her chest. Was that physically possible? Because it certainly felt like he'd just handed her the keys to the kingdom without so much as doing reconnaissance. Trust. Had her ex ever trusted her? Beyond believing his nightly dinners weren't poisoned, she wasn't sure. He hadn't trusted her to choose her own outfits or to lead in the bedroom. He hadn't trusted her to stay in touch with her friends and family. Or maybe he just hadn't trusted himself. But Elias... This was a man who earned respect and expected others to do the same. The idea that she'd met his qualifications added to the lightness of knowing they'd survived a killer. Though she wasn't sure what she'd done to join that small club.

The skin across his stomach was smooth and warm and urged her to linger. Muscle flexed and released under her ministrations, and she couldn't deny there was something wholly superficial in the heat clawing up her neck and into her face. He was attractive—no argument there—and

Sayles almost didn't recognize that tug in her lower belly. It'd been so long since she'd let herself notice another man. And Elias was definitely hard to ignore. "Almost done. Just need to apply a new dressing. Does it hurt?"

"Not so much anymore." The gravel in his words eased. Softer.

She stretched one hand across his midsection to hold the new gauze in place and fought with the roll of medical tape. The burn of his attention spread lower, raising goose bumps along her arms and waking her nerves to the point she couldn't focus on what her hands were doing at all.

"I got it." Taking the roll from her, he sectioned out four pieces, handing them off one by one. They worked together to press the dressing into place.

"I'll take another look at it in a few hours to make sure there's no signs of infection. Until then, try to keep it dry and don't jar it." Repacking her supplies back into the kit, she swallowed the urge to close those inches between them. To lose herself in him all over again. That deep-rooted need would have to wait. The killer had been watching them since they'd stepped onto the trail. There was no telling if he'd attack again, and she wasn't going to distract Elias from doing his job. Sayles rushed through organizing her pack and inventorying what was left. Seemed the killer had only taken her multi-tool. Probably in case she decided to stab him with it while he forced her help. "We have a couple hours of until sunset, but I'm not in the right headspace to keep pushing. We'd be better served getting some rest until tomorrow morning."

Because Elias had been right. This wasn't over. Surviving a serial killer hadn't done a damn bit of good. He was still out there.

A calloused hand covered hers. Pinning her in place. Elias slipped a finger beneath her chin, directing her to meet his gaze. Understanding and a hint of concern etched his expression where she'd only been met with frustration and disappointment from her ex. She wasn't used to this. This consideration. She didn't know what to do with it. "I'm not going to let him get to you again. I give you my word."

"I'm not sure that's something you can promise." Against her best defenses, her chin wobbled as the burn of tears crested, but she wouldn't break. Not because of the bastard who'd shoved her off the trail. She wouldn't let him haunt her. Ever. "You were right before. He wanted me to lead him to the end of the Narrows at Big Spring to cut west, but I don't think he's as experienced as we assumed. He'd started suffering from acute mountain sickness, getting dizzy the higher we climbed."

Elias let his hand drop away from her face, and she instantly regretted the loss of connection. "Did he say anything else?"

"Told me his name is Patrick, but I can't be sure he wasn't lying." A heaviness she'd refused to acknowledge seeped into her muscles, into her bones. The adrenaline brought on by sheer survival had left her raw and unstable. The crash was coming. It was only a matter of how long until she turned into a psychopath. "And he certainly liked the moniker you'd given him. Went straight to his head. But I didn't get the impression he's doing this for fun. He had a plan."

"What kind of plan?" He sat back on his heels, every inch of his muscled frame fighting against his sweats and T-shirt. So unlike the suits and ties and slacks she'd been expected to iron up until a few months ago. Her ex never would've felt comfortable in a tent this small. Or camping in general.

Sayles hauled her pack to the side of the tent, out of the way, and summoned everything she had left into crawling into her sleeping bag. The rough material aggravated the cuts across her hands, and she fisted them close to her chest. "He wouldn't tell me. Said he had his reasons for killing those people. I tried..."

"You did good, Sayles." His voice sounded close. "I'm proud of how hard you fought today. Not everyone can say they survived like you did."

A swell of emotion worked to reinvigorate her mission, but her eyes slipped closed. Dragged into near unconsciousness within seconds. She couldn't get settled. Like there was something she was forgetting. She rolled onto her side, then onto her back and repeated the cycle all over again.

Movement registered behind her, the rustle of his sleeping bag as he climbed into it too loud despite the rush of the river mere feet from their position. It wasn't until Elias secured his arm around her waist and pulled her flush against his front that her nervous system released her from the fight. "Get some rest. I'll keep watch. I won't let him take you from me again."

The words carved through layered defensiveness and flipped some kind of switch in her brain that told her it was safe. That he would protect her. He would fight for her.

And she drifted off to sleep.

Chapter Eighteen

There was no going back.

Elias made quick work of packing their gear before setting onto the trail. Muscles he hadn't known existed ached as he grabbed for his pack and took that first step back onto the Narrows. They'd cleared the tent and set out in record time, barely saying more than a few words to each other. Working in comfortable silence. He'd learned Sayles's morning routine over the past couple of days, and she'd silently fixed his backpack Tetris game with a smile. Yeah. Nearly dying tended to bring people closer.

They'd reached a comfortable partnership. So different from the years he'd been assigned to work cases with Grant. This was…pleasant. And Sayles wasn't trying to suffocate him with too much body spray.

Sayles handed off one of her protein bars. They hadn't eaten nearly enough in the past two days compared to the effort it'd taken to come this far, and Elias shoved the bar down with a few swigs of water, then got into his own supplies for a sloppy peanut butter sandwich. The bread had been squished during moments of survival and panic, and condensation had built up in the baggie, but his stomach didn't care in the least. He caught Sayles going for seconds, too. As if she understood what lay ahead.

Blue sky touched with a hint of wispy clouds at the edges slowly flared to life as they traversed Wall Street Corridor. The morning crest of sun reflected off 1,500-foot walls closing in on either side of them, merely twenty-two feet across, and cast rays of purple down weather-worn rock. Evidence of drainage stained blinding red stone in white streaks and dark patches. The canyon itself curved, cutting off any chance of scouting the trail ahead of them. They were going into this section of the trail blind. At a disadvantage. The only comfort was their killer would be, too. There was no escaping this portion of the trail if another flash flood hit. The Hitchhiker Killer would be caught right along with them. Hell, a storm might even flush him out. But the weather seemed to be cooperating this morning.

Sayles arched her head back onto her shoulders, slowing a few feet ahead of him. A body-wide sigh released the tension in her neck. "This view never ceases to amaze me. There's just something about this specific spot before heading into Wall Street Corridor that gets to me."

He couldn't argue. While he'd never been an outdoor explorer, even when the other kids in his neighborhood growing up went out on hikes together and spent every minute figuring out how to, Elias felt a sense of…peace here. Of soul-deep quiet. He couldn't say he'd still feel that way if it weren't just him and Sayles on this trail, but something in his chest released as he took in the natural monument overhead. The rough edges of rock, the smoothness of where rain and a natural waterfall had rubbed away the harshness, the differing colors of wear and age. The river itself had quieted through this section and reflected that same blue of the sky above. He couldn't remember a time he'd allowed himself to slow down and just…be. He couldn't describe the beauty of this place. Made even more extravagant by the woman urging him to notice it. "I can see why you're out here as much as you are."

Though he wasn't sure he'd step foot on this trail again once the investigation was closed. In a little under two days, they'd nearly drowned—twice—been shot at, he'd been stabbed by a tree and watched Sayles go over the edge of a cliff. He'd just about soaked up all the nature he could handle. But turning back wasn't an option. Not with the killer still out there. With the improbability of getting a signal out of the canyon, NPS had no reason to believe they required assistance or rescue, which meant he and Sayles were on their own for now.

"At first it was a way to escape. To hide from the gossip that still followed me. To avoid any chance one of his friends may want to do him a favor, even from prison." Her smile didn't reach her eyes. As much as she wanted to play off the trauma she'd survived, Elias understood it would always be there. Always shape her choices, her relationships, her way of thinking. It would determine who she allowed to get close and bar anyone she deemed unsafe from experiencing the fighter beneath that guarded gaze, but damn, she was a sight. In her element. Worth every pain, every second of fear. "The more I came out here, the less it became about the hiding, and the more I found myself. Just hours in my own head, forcing myself to face what'd happened. And figuring out who I wanted to be next. It's probably weird to consider a trail like the Narrows capable of saving my life after everything we've been through these past couple of days, but that's what happened."

Sayles set that green gaze on him, and he could see it, feel it. The life and the brilliance bleeding to the surface, past her defenses. This wasn't the park ranger who'd built walls to avoid getting too close to her cohort or make herself small enough the FBI wouldn't notice. The mask had come off, leaving nothing but the woman who'd ensnared him from the beginning, and he didn't have the discipline to look away.

No. He wanted to stay right here. Just the two of them and these cliffs. Pretend nothing else existed outside of this perfect bubble they'd created together. In another life, he'd just be one of the millions of hikers who came here each year and she would be a ranger working to keep him from doing something stupid and dying on this trail. Because…paperwork. Of course, he'd notice her right away, and she'd politely stir conversation to the specifics of the park and her job. She might not be interested in him at all, but he'd keep trying. Ask her to take that leap of faith and trust in something again.

"Do you have something like that back home?" The spell broke as Sayles guided them farther upstream. Water rippled away from her charge forward and collided with the base of the cliffs on either side. "Something that makes you happy?"

Was it too cheesy to tell her that over these past couple days she'd made him happy? That their back-and-forth had kept him from ruminating on all the mistakes he'd made in the course of his last case? That she'd resurrected some part of him that wanted a partner in crime that didn't come with Cheetos fingers and burping the alphabet in a too-hot FBI-issued car? Yes. Too cheesy.

Elias gripped his pack tighter to counter the hole spreading through his chest. He'd managed to tie both straps together to make it easier to carry but still couldn't strap it to his back. "My job. Bringing killers to justice makes me pretty happy. Knowing that they won't hurt anyone else because I was able to put it to a stop."

"You don't sound happy about that." Her retort didn't come with the expected judgment or disappointment.

He couldn't stop his laugh at seeing the pinch between her brows. As if he'd personally given her reason to react on his behalf. "What do I sound like?"

Sayles slowed her pace. Seemingly giving herself time to form the words without offending him altogether. "Like you've accepted your fate, and there's nothing you can do to change it."

He pulled up short. A tug started in his gut. In a way, she was right. He'd never imagined another life for himself than the one he had now. Maybe a few changes in the details, but this—working for the FBI—was where he belonged. Where he felt his purpose. "My dad served as a highway patrol officer for thirty years. Everything I know about law enforcement came from him before I was fifteen years old. It's in my blood, and the second I turned eighteen, I applied to the local police academy looking to follow in his footsteps. I wanted to be just like him. Protecting people, making sure the bad guys didn't get away."

Guiding them deeper into the corridor, Sayles kept at his side instead of ahead. As though she knew the cost of giving up this small part of himself. As she had.

"He worked hard. Gone every week on shift, driving up

and down the state, mostly pulling people over for speeding. My mom and I would see him on the weekends, and I looked forward to every Friday night when he walked through our front door with stories from his week. I'd wait in the kitchen with a chilled beer ready for him and a pizza on the way. After a while it just became our tradition." Elias remembered every single story. Held on to them as best he could. It was the only way he could think to honor his father's dedication to the job. To turning Elias into the man he was today, whether he'd been there or not.

"Until one Friday he didn't come home."

Sayles's attention settled along his left side. "What happened?"

"He'd pulled over a suspected drunk driver on I-80, outside of a little nothing town you'd never heard of. Nothing but desert around. Multiple calls had been made about the truck hitting both lines, cutting people off, going slow, then speeding up. Typical driving under the influence." Except the stop had been anything but routine. "He was sideswiped by another vehicle. Killed instantly."

"I'm so sorry." Genuine regret laced her words and tunneled through him, straight through his skin, muscle and bone, and settled in his soul.

"It's one of the risks of being highway patrol. Motorists, no matter how much driving experience they have, aren't paying as much attention as they should. He knew that and wanted to do the job anyway. That was just the kind of man he was. Saw a need and worked to fill it, even if it meant putting himself in danger." Because who else would step up to do the right thing? His father had made sure Elias had absorbed that mentality from a young age. "We got the call he'd been in an accident, and the paramedics hadn't gotten to him in time. We found out later the driver who'd hit him hadn't bothered to stick around, and the one my dad had pulled over had taken off."

"They just left him there?" Her voice wobbled, and Elias couldn't hold himself back from looking at her anymore. His sorrow had become her own, as if she were trying to shoulder some of the weight.

"Another driver called it in a couple minutes later. Tried to help him, but there was nothing they could do." Tension radiated from his shoulders down his spine. "Later on, we learned the truth of what'd happened. Once I was in the academy, I convinced my dad's former supervisor to show me the dashcam footage from his car that day. Turned out the driver he'd pulled over hadn't been drunk. He'd had a woman in the car with him. Someone he'd kidnapped. She'd been trying to fight him off while they barreled down the freeway, and the vehicle that'd hit him was his partner."

Sayles's jaw slackened. "Your dad was trying to help her?"

"He didn't get the chance, but I think he realized what was happening when he stepped up to the car. He was in a position to help, and he would've done anything to get her out of there safely.

"I'm not sure I had much of a choice about joining the academy after that. I wanted to keep him with me, help people, and falling into law enforcement seemed like the right way to do it. I worked for Las Vegas Metro police department for a few years before turning my sights on the FBI. So, yeah. Being an agent makes me happy. Gives me a reason to keep going."

"What happened to the drivers?" She didn't need to

voice the rest of that question. Worried about what'd happened to the woman in the car.

"They were never found. The license plates on both vehicles had been stolen. A search of local auto body shops never turned up anything concrete. State police closed their investigation three months after the incident without any new leads. We were told to move on. That that's what my dad would've wanted." But he'd known better. He'd known his father never would've given up had Elias been in his position. His own regret soured at the back of his mouth. "But I'm still looking."

Her eyes widened at that. A secret he'd never told anyone but his mother before now. Not even Grant. "What will you do if you find them?"

He didn't bother lying. "I'll make them pay."

Chapter Nineteen

Her heart hurt.

Along with the rest of her.

She could feel the pain rippling off Elias as he'd re-lived the last few memories of his dad. It was a wonder he hadn't let that loss corrupt him. Turn him bitter and guarded. As she had. How had he done it? How had he managed to keep himself grounded when all she'd wanted to do was run, to hide and forget all those broken pieces of herself?

Flecks of water caressed her face as they passed be-neath a tendril of water snaking down the rock canyon wall. He was going to make the people responsible for his father's death pay. Because Elias was the kind of man who never gave up on the ones he cared about. He'd proven that coming after her, hadn't he? Loyal. Warm. Dependable. She wasn't sure her ex had ever possessed those qualities, and maybe she'd blinded herself to the red flags. Maybe her standards for affection had been so low that the small amount she'd received from her ex had felt like a privi-lege instead of a given, but that wasn't the case anymore.

Elias had shown her that in the span of mere days as they'd worked together, survived together, saved each other. It was in the way he'd treated her as an equal and trusted her experience. How he'd let her take the lead and speak her mind. Respect. He respected her, and the realization imbued her with a sense of power. And desire. For possibility and change and…hope. It was an odd feeling. The shift that came with looking toward the future instead of living in the past.

Her ex was still out there, though she'd been granted a divorce by the state considering law enforcement couldn't find him. He would always shadow her every thought, every choice, but she was so tired of letting him win. And that was exactly what she'd done by running from Colorado after her release and the courts had settled on her wrongful imprisonment. She'd let him win by giving up contact with her family, by pushing her away from her friends and her home, by not fighting back.

"I hope you find them. The people who killed your dad." She meant it. Wanting that closure for Elias, even though she couldn't have it for herself. To see her ex pay for what he'd done to her. They were nearly through Wall Street Corridor. The sun's rays descended along rough outcroppings and sharp edges of the canyon wall. Her body temperature dropped as they crossed into the shade, then immediately spiked entering the sunlight. "I know what it's like to not have closure. To wish you could change things."

It wasn't a great feeling, succumbing to a feeling created solely by a man determined to give up her entire identity for him. For nothing in return.

"You'll get yours." Elias's confidence fought to soak into her, would if she let it, but she'd become all too accustomed to wearing a mask. A thick layer of protection against any and all feeling. It'd been the only way to get through those horrible months behind bars, to not hope. But the federal agent at her side had slowly started dismantling the darkness she'd lived in these past few months. Bringing with him a hint of light so small she hadn't recognized it for what it was. A raft. He winked at her. Still playful after everything they'd survived. She hoped he never lost that ability. "It might not be today or next week, but sooner or later, he's going to make a mistake. People like your ex think too highly of themselves. Think they're smarter than the rest of us. Most of the time to their own downfall."

Why did she get the feeling Elias would ensure her ex's arrest if given the opportunity? Sayles didn't let herself follow that thought down the rabbit hole too much further. If she was being honest with herself, the comparisons she'd drawn—between her ex and Elias—were another added layer of protection. Trying to find similarities. A reason to shut whatever this was between them down before it had a chance to get under her skin. But he'd saved her. When she'd had nothing more than a palm-size rock and a knowledge of the park to her advantage against the Hitchhiker Killer, he'd saved her where her ex had purposefully tried to destroy her. And fear that had nothing to do with the trail and everything to do with that distinction slithered into awareness.

"I think I would like to see that." Maybe she could somehow get a front-row seat in the courthouse. Just to watch her ex betray himself as effectively as he'd betrayed her. He deserved it. For what he'd done. For what he'd turned her into.

"Didn't take you for the vengeful type." Elias dragged his feet through the chilled waters rising to their calves, flashing her that smile quickly highlighting her days. "I like it."

"Thanks. I think." Her self-critic—moderately created by the man who'd framed her for murder—fought against that compliment. If that was what it was. Sayles shut down the inclination to shrink. Elias liked something about her, and the comment hadn't come with a hint of sarcasm. She…believed him. Maybe her willingness to watch her ex go down in flames of his own making wasn't the only thing, either. Wow. He'd really screwed her up, hadn't he? Convinced her she wasn't worth complimenting, that she was nothing without him. How was it even months later she was fighting against all these little mechanisms and habits she'd picked up to cope throughout her marriage? Why couldn't she just let it go? And why the hell couldn't she give herself a break and accept it would take time?

"You good?" Elias tapped the back of his hand against her arm. Bringing her back to the moment. Pulling her out of the spiral with mere touch. Just as he had in the tent, dragging her body against his. Giving her permission to use him in whatever capacity she'd needed to get through what they'd suffered.

It'd been enough. She'd dropped into unconsciousness within seconds with him pressed against her. That was all it'd taken. Because she'd felt…safe. For the first time in a long time, she hadn't even thought about putting a weapon beneath her pillow or triple-checking the zipper on her tent. She hadn't startled awake in the middle of the night at the slightest sound that didn't fit her surroundings. There'd only been Elias, who'd held her throughout the night as though he'd needed her as much as she'd needed him. And it'd felt right. Like a puzzle piece she'd been missing for months had finally clicked into place. "I'm good."

And it wasn't the same lie she'd been telling her fellow rangers or Risner or anyone else who'd bothered to check in out of a warped sense of obligation. The heaviness she'd adapted to since leaving Colorado didn't have the same hold on her as it had a few days ago. Because of him. "Thinking about what happens after you catch this killer."

"What do you mean?" Elias made a good effort to focus on the path he carved through the river.

"I mean you kissed me yesterday." Tightening her grip around her pack's straps, she tried to counter the ball of anxiety in the pit of her stomach. It was no use. "Do you normally go around kissing your partners during an investigation?"

"Grant hasn't complained." His laugh charged through her, sweeping the last remnants of apprehension from her veins. He shook his head. "No. I don't just go around kissing people on cases. Though, can you blame me for wanting to kiss you? You're freaking formidable hanging off the edge of a cliff. Anyone else in your position would've given up, but you fought."

She didn't have an answer for that, but the beaten-down ghost of her past self preened. Hell, she needed a life. Friends, hobbies, dreams—all the things her ex had systematically cut her off from. Lila, her roommate, didn't count, and could she really consider hiking the Narrows every weekend a hobby if it was technically her job? As for dreams… It'd been a long time since she'd considered what would come next. Since she'd allowed herself to hope it wouldn't be taken away. "Oh. Well, I haven't…um, kissed anyone since…before I was arrested. Or dated any-one. Or just generally given anyone the impression I am a nice person, but I want to know what you think it meant."

"You mean if I want to kiss you again." Elias halted right there in the middle of the river. The mere words out of his mouth—the idea of his mouth on hers again—coiled something low in her belly. "Yeah. I think I do."

"Why?" She hadn't meant to ask, but there it was. All of the doubt and self-hatred and disappointment in her-self that'd built up since two officers had shown up at her door to arrest her for her ex's murder. Doubt that she'd make it through, self-hatred for staying with the bastard as long as she had and the disappointment for not seeing who he'd really been before it was too late. A rawness spread through her. Why? Why did a man like Elias—tough-minded, accomplished and honor-bound—want anything to do with the hot mess in front of him?

He closed that short distance between them, looking far too put together than he deserved after what they'd survived. "You want to know what I see in you?"

Did that make her needy? Wanting to know who in their right mind would look at her and see something other than a broken thing that had no chance of living a normal life again? Her mouth dried.

"I see a woman who isn't afraid to express her very strong opinions." His smile cracked another layer of armor she'd relied on over the past couple of years. "You never seem to run out of energy, which makes me think you're some kind of witch sent to put my outdoor skills to shame." Elias skimmed calloused fingertips along her forearm, then over the pulse in her wrist. The contact was enough to shove those fears back into the box at the back of her mind where they belonged. "Despite the front you put on, I think you feel more than anyone else I've ever met. You're the kind of person who will never forget or forgive the slights against her, and I admire that about you. I admire your outright determination to become someone you're proud of, who will never take abuse or manipulation again and who will put herself at risk to protect others from suffering what you went through."

Six years of marriage and her ex had never bothered to really get to know her, but this man had somehow worked past her defenses. She couldn't dislodge the swell of emotion in her throat. "You see all that after only two days together?"

"I saw it the moment I met you." Dropping his hand from hers, Elias waited for her to make the next move. Choice. It was always a choice with him.

They were coming up on the four-mile point, a marker that should've taken no more than three and a half hours to reach on a good day, but the park itself seemed to be turning against them. Not to mention the killer determined to escape. Wynopits Mountain demanded attention over the wall of the canyon to the east. One mile more and they'd reach Big Spring, where the Narrows officially ended. Where the Hitchhiker Killer had wanted her to take him, but her instincts told her there was something more to his final destination. Not that he'd just wanted out of the park, but that there might be something there he needed.

"The killer—Patrick—wanted me to get him to Big Spring before the FBI could catch up with him." Sayles swiped at her face with a renewed energy singing through her. Of possibility and hope. "I think we should get there first."

Chapter Twenty

He could still taste her.

On his tongue, in his soul.

Sayles Green had barged into his life without mercy and taken him for everything he had. She'd picked up their pace after he'd agreed to her plan to head the Hitchhiker Killer off, but they still had to fight the river's current with every step. She never faltered. Each foot strike more sure than the last. It was a testament to her determination to prove she was more than the woman who'd been conned by someone she believed had loved her, and he couldn't help but follow in her footsteps. To think he had a chance of escaping the past as she had. Of fighting back.

His body ached, particularly the tops of his thighs as he battled against the upstream current. Floodwaters had spread out and down the trail, but the river still parted around his waist. It was a fight, plain and simple, and they had no idea how far ahead the killer had gotten in the time it'd taken him and Sayles to recover since yesterday. Every second counted. They couldn't waste a single one of them.

They'd navigated through Wall Street Corridor and lived to tell the tale on the other side. If another flash flood hit, they had an actual chance of making it out alive. It was the threats he couldn't predict that simmered beneath his skin now. His entire career centered on seeing all the ways an investigation could go south and giving himself the advantage in the end, but he couldn't discard the possibility he'd missed something here. Potentially putting Sayles back in the killer's sights. Not an option he could live with.

"You're awfully quiet for once." Sayles dared a glance back in his direction, her face slightly flushed, out of breath. She was exerting herself, burning through whatever energy she had left over after the attack from yesterday. While they'd both managed to get to sleep in that cramped tent last night, she'd tossed and tensed throughout the night. No matter how tightly he'd held her.

They'd packed supplies for three days, and neither of them wanted to acknowledge what would happen when they ran out, though he didn't doubt it was one of the main concerns on her mind. Always planning ahead. Always looking for the escape.

"Is that your way of telling me you don't enjoy my company?" The retort slipped from him easily enough, but he'd left his humor a few hundred yards back. "Something about this case isn't sitting right."

"What do you mean?" She'd turned forward again, never one to lead them off the path or put their safety at risk. He'd been the one to make that choice, to prioritize catching a killer above both of their lives. A mistake he wouldn't make again. If it came right down to it, he'd make sure Sayles got out. He owed her that.

"The killer's motive." It was the key to this entire case. He could feel it, but nothing they'd gathered so far during this investigation hinted as to what drove the Hitchhiker Killer. "He murdered four motorists between California and Utah. Then a random hiker here in the park. Nothing connects any of the victims. They're a mixture of male and female, married and single, with no common backgrounds. Not even the same makes or models of vehicles. He wipes down every car he's in to make sure he doesn't leave his prints behind. Our forensic techs haven't been able to collect any DNA to identify him. What's he running from?"

"What if he's not running from something?" Sayles chanced another glance over her shoulder, giving him a glimpse of brightness in her gaze. "What if he's trying to get somewhere?"

Elias had to focus on his next steps to keep himself from face-planting in the middle of the river. "What makes you say that?"

"Nothing. Never mind." She shook her head, pushing them forward. "It probably doesn't mean anything."

His heart jerked in his chest. Reaching out, he secured his fingers around her elbow and dragged her to a stop. He could see it then, the signs of a person who'd been convinced she'd meant nothing. That she wasn't important enough or deserving of someone's time, least of all when it came to matters of an investigation. Elias's teeth protested as a burn of rage at the bastard responsible for ever making this woman feel less than took over. "Of the two of us you're the only one who's had a real conversation with this guy. I want to know what you think."

"I just… I got the impression there's something waiting for him at the end of the trail." Her shoulder rose on a deep inhale, but Sayles refused to look at him. "Like he didn't so much want to escape, but rather get to something or someone waiting for him there. It's ridiculous, I know. I'm probably reading too deep into it. He'd threatened me, and I was scared—"

"No." Her body heat seeped into his hand, kept him grounded and calm in the face of the chaos and confusion closing in around them. He wasn't sure he'd ever experienced that because of another person. At least not since his dad had been killed. "During my training, instructors and training officers would always encourage recruits to look at facts and evidence. They didn't want us making assumptions or taking an investigation off course because of our bias. Logically, it makes sense, but some of the best calls I've made in cases like this are from listening to my gut. That instinct has saved lives over the course of my career, and I trust yours. Especially out here."

She wanted to brush his reasoning off, to pretend that she was nothing and nobody to him and this investigation, but that just wasn't the truth. In a matter of days, she'd taken up more of his thoughts than he was willing to admit and sure as hell never would to Grant or his special agent in charge back at the home office. "I'm not in law enforcement. I'm not trained to theorize killers' motives."

"But you know people." That was how trauma worked. The terror of it could never be erased. Not from the victim's nervous system and not as the brain physically rewired itself to stay on alert and absorb the slightest shift or possibility of a threat. "You know what they're capable of and how to read the smallest signs that something isn't right. You've been doing it for years, and I trust you, Sayles."

His words hit a barrier in her emotions, as he'd expected. Her bastard of an ex had done a thorough job in tearing her down, but Elias wanted nothing more than to erase that pain. To show her how to believe in herself again. As she'd done for him without even realizing it. In the way she'd relaxed in his arms the two nights they'd camped in that too-small tent. In the way she'd challenged him to reconsider his priorities in life, to allow something other than his job to consume him. In the way she'd shown him what real strength looked like as she'd fought for her life instead of waiting for anyone else to save her. He shifted his weight between both legs, leveling his gaze with hers. "You talked with him. He told you things about himself, so what would a man like Patrick kill five people for if not to escape arrest?"

The muscles in her jaw ticked as she considered him for a few moments, unsure of herself and her own theory, but he noted the moment she decided to take a chance. "I think he's looking for someone."

Pride heated through him, and Elias stood a bit taller. There she was. The woman he imagined she'd been before her ex had gotten a hold of her. One forged of single-mindedness and mission, who wouldn't let anyone stop her from getting what she wanted. "Do you know who?"

"He didn't even tell me that much. I just..." Doubt bled from her gaze, leaving nothing behind but a flare of excitement. How long had she been waiting for someone to believe her? To take her word for it? To see her? "I have a feeling it's someone important."

"All right." Elias nodded once. It was a vague detail that could risk the investigation if she ended up being wrong, but one they didn't really have a choice other than to take. He'd meant what he'd said. He trusted her. He wasn't sure when it'd started. Maybe when she'd hauled him out of the raging river's path during that first flash flood. Maybe when she'd called his name from the edge of that cliff, telling him she trusted him to help. Maybe when he'd kissed her in the aftermath and something in him had snapped at coming so close to losing her. All it meant was she'd been right about him. There was more out there than his job and running himself into the ground case after case. More to live for than the mistakes he'd made and the people he'd let down, including his dad. "Then we proceed on that assumption."

"Why?" There was that question again. Her need to understand why he believed her above his own training, why he'd even consider trusting her when no one else had.

Elias didn't have an answer. At least not one that would satisfy the doubt she'd lived with for so long. Stepping into her personal space, he framed her chin with his thumb and index finger and pressed his mouth to hers. Not as he had on that trail they'd left behind, full of desperation for something real and solid to hold on to. But intentionally forcing himself to slow down, to feel every sensation and sweep of her lips against his. And his defenses crumbled. Desire, unlike anything he'd experienced with all those meaningless dates, surged through his veins. He wanted to be the one she trusted, the one who cracked that careful control she'd put into place to protect herself against any further hurt. Coaxing her lips apart with the tip of his tongue, Elias tightened his hold on her chin as she jerked against him. Then she softened into him, opened for him. Allowed him to take control, and his whole body shuddered in response.

Hell, it wasn't his first kiss, and it sure as hell wasn't hers considering she'd been married—it wasn't even their first kiss with each other—but it felt as though something new was building between them now. A bridge between damaged souls who'd gone through this life long enough without each other and had finally come home.

She'd fisted her cut and bruised hands in his shirt as

though afraid the river would sweep him away, but he wasn't going anywhere. Not now and not after he closed this case. He wasn't sure how it would work between her here in Zion and him based out of Las Vegas, but a few hundred miles between them wasn't going to make a damn bit of difference. He'd make sure of it.

A screech echoed off the canyon walls, and Elias broke the kiss to assess the oncoming threat.

Spotting a lone turkey fanning his brown-gray wings in a sliver of sunshine upriver.

Elias blinked to clear his head. Hard to do when all he could think about was Sayles. "Either I'm severely malnourished and dehydrated, or there's a turkey sunbathing on that rock."

She craned her head over one shoulder but kept her hands locked in his shirt. "That's Frank. He lives in the park."

"You named it." Of course she had. His stomach growled, reminding him he hadn't eaten since they'd set out a couple hours ago. "I don't suppose we're allowed to eat him."

Sayles smacked her hand against his chest. Almost hard enough to knock him off-balance. Thankfully she wouldn't be witnessing that blunder. "You can't eat mascots, but if I'm being honest, turkey sounds really good right now."

"I'll get you some when we're back at the visitors' center." He just wouldn't tell Frank about that. "So tell me, Ranger Green, how do we get to Big Spring before the killer does?"

Chapter Twenty-One

She could've gone another lifetime without seeing this trail again.

They'd taken a gamble in hiking the 1,500-foot incline that crested the west canyon wall hiding the Narrows in its base. Her toes slipped on the next ascent, nearly launching her back into Elias. His hands framed her hips as she righted herself, keeping her from falling, but the rains from the past couple of days dissolved any sort of traction. One wrong move, and they'd lose the game the Hitchhiker Killer had set in motion. She had to be more careful. Breath crushed from her chest and aggravated the bruising along her ribs. "Thanks."

"I was hoping never to do this again." Elias struggled to even his breathing at her back, and she only hoped they hadn't ascended too fast and triggered altitude sickness. He was assigned out of the Las Vegas FBI office. Well below the park's elevation. "Can't promise I won't have a heart attack before we get to the top."

"Almost there." Using the goat trail gave them the slimmest chance of getting ahead of the killer by avoiding the river's current and any debris and obstacles in their way if he'd kept to the official Narrows trail. It was the only option they had despite the anxiety-tense muscle strain memories of yesterday tightening down her spine, but she'd never hiked the rim of the canyon. Her knowledge extended to the main trails in and around Zion. Elias had hired her as a guide, but this was foreign territory where any number of dangers could bite them in the ass.

Sun blinded her a split second before the ground under her feet evened out. Clear skies stretched as far as the eye could see. Miles and miles of barren red rock spread out before her in every direction, and a lightness she'd initially felt on the trails prickled the hair on the back of her neck. Wispy clouds played against the velvet of the sky, almost dancing on the breeze that untucked her hair from its crude braid. This. This was what she'd chased all those months after leaving Colorado. A fullness she couldn't find anywhere else. Except she'd felt it down in that canyon, with Elias's mouth pressed to hers. With every stroke of his tongue and shift of his hand on her face.

The kiss had been sweet and coaxing and freeing all in the same breath. Unlike anything she'd experienced before and a reminder of how little she'd been cared for in the past. But the anger—the disappointment—wasn't there anymore. She waited for the shame to rear its ugly head. It never showed, and Sayles didn't know what to think about that. What to do with that.

She explored that sensation, reveled in the emptiness the view and the man at her side provided. She'd survived the past couple of years off spite and anger alone, but now there was nothing but a hole where it'd slept. Because of Elias. No. Not emptiness. Something lighter that took her a few seconds to feel out. Brighter. Filling. It'd slipped in without her notice and meticulously replaced the hurt she held on to to keep everyone at arm's length.

Hope. That was what this was. So foreign and unusual but stronger than the remnants of a lost life she'd tried holding on to for herself. That pain and betrayal she'd believed protected her were nothing but scraps compared to the solid hold Elias had offered. A lifeline she hadn't seen until now. Where she didn't have to shoulder the past alone and could let herself imagine a future. Dream and plan and thrive. With him.

"Wow." Elias kept his distance, not willing to crowd her on the too-narrow trail though his massive frame threatened to tip her right over the edge.

"Yeah." They weren't shaken by the same view. His amazement came from their physical perspective. Hers from inside. She planted her boots. It'd be easy to let the lack of guardrails and the sheer elevation get to her, but right now, she felt as though she were flying. Free. The river tendrilled and curved below them, but she couldn't make out any distinguishing signs of the killer. He'd managed to escape them once. She couldn't let him get away again. Couldn't be responsible for the devastation he would cause if she failed.

Crackling reached her ears, raising her senses on to high alert. There. A voice? Broken but there if she listened hard enough. Understanding hit. Sayles wrenched her pack free and swung it around. Diving her hand inside, she hit the solid casing of her emergency radio. "We're out of the canyon. Radio waves can reach us here."

Pressing the push-to-talk button, she called into the visitors' center. They could reach Risner—or anyone else—from this elevation. "This is Ranger Green. Hello? Can you hear me?"

Stillness flooded through her and Elias as they waited,

barely willing to make a noise that might drown out any response. She tried again. "Green to VC. Is anyone there? Risner? Hello?"

"Green? Copy." For perhaps the first time ever, Risner's nasally response flooded her with a sense of relief. "We've been trying to get to you for two days. We thought we'd lost you and Agent Broyles. Where the hell are you?"

Sayles closed her eyes against the drugging sensation of contact with the outside world. Nearly pressing the radio to her face, she leaned against its metal casing. "Four miles in the Narrows, closing in on Big Spring. Damn, it's good to hear your voice." She'd never admit that to anyone. Ever. Least of all Risner after today. "We're still in pursuit of the killer. Lucky to be alive after those flash floods."

Elias silently beckoned for the radio, and she handed it off. "Risner, this is Agent Broyles. I need to speak with the agent there with you at the visitors' center."

"Agent Marques is here. Hold on. I'll put you on." Static crackled over the airwaves for more than a minute before another voice broke through. "Elias, what the hell, man. Where have you been? I've been trying to get a hold of you since yesterday afternoon. We've got reports of flash floods in the Narrows. Search and rescue is waiting for the flooding to clear so they can come in and get you. Are you all right?"

His gaze locked on hers as he raised the radio to his mouth. "That doesn't matter. Listen, we're closing in on this guy. Do you have any updates from your end that can help us?"

"Yeah, yeah. Just a sec. Let me get my notes." Her partner looked as though he was about to crumple the radio's casing as they waited. The sun had already started making its afternoon arch across the sky. They would lose daylight in the next couple of hours, and there was nowhere to camp on this trail. Not to mention a single source of light to ensure they didn't step straight off the cliff face. "I searched the van our unsub stole from the last interstate victim, but the entire setup had been wiped down as we expected. I managed to contact the victim's family and send them photos of the van to see if they might notice anything missing or out of place."

Elias raised the radio again, quick and efficient before lowering it back between them. All the while refusing to take his attention off her. Sweat built at his temple, and it was then she realized how much protection the canyon had offered. Now? Now they were exposed. Vulnerable. Easy targets. "And?"

"Turns out she was an avid climber. Ropes, chalk, carabiners, the works. She was making the trip across the country to climb the national parks, including Zion." The radio cut out. "—must've taken all her gear."

Pinching the radio and raising it back to his mouth, Elias narrowed his gaze on her. "What would he want with climbing gear?"

"Zion has over two hundred and fifty documented free climbs, but none in the Narrows." This didn't make sense. Sayles mentally ran through the possibilities.

"There's more." Agent Marques—Grant—waited a beat, and Sayles's own impatience charged to the surface. "The victim discovered by your ranger lady at the bottom of the trail. He was traveling with a group of friends from Texas. Four of them, but two days ago they'd split up to take on the trails they personally wanted to hike. Our vic went straight for the Narrows that morning. The other three came to the visitors' center after the park had been emptied. No one had heard from him, you know, because he was dead, but what they really wanted to tell me was that our latest victim never went anywhere without his handgun."

Sayles shook her head. "There wasn't a handgun on the body when I found it."

Her partner straightened. Every inch the federal agent he was supposed to be. The one she'd feared would break the last dregs of her soul if she gave him the chance. Gone was the easy smile and the banter, the warmth he'd supplied in the middle of the night with her pressed against his chest. This was the trained agent who'd vowed to find his father's killer, and Sayles had the inclination to back away. And that lightness she'd felt a few minutes ago faltered. "Because the killer took it."

The Hitchhiker Killer—Patrick, or whoever he was— had a gun. She turned her attention back to the river below, somehow managing to take an even breath as her heart threatened to beat out of her chest.

Elias and his partner's conversation distorted into short commands and faded responses. She didn't have the energy to follow along as pieces of this messed-up puzzle started falling into place. A stolen handgun, climbing gear, a blurred target at the end of the trail. Each seemingly dangerous enough on its own, but together? Sayles shuddered as footsteps thundered through the slight ringing in her ears.

Elias. "Grant is going to go back and talk with our forensics teams to double-check all the other vehicles our unsub stole to see if anything is missing from the victim's bags or trunks."

"We should keep moving. We only have a few more hours of daylight and another mile to cover before we reach Big Spring." She didn't have the capacity for much else, dependent on the feel of the trail under her feet, the reliability of her balance. Connection to the very park she'd given herself over to these past few months. Sayles took that initial step, but Elias's hand threaded between her arm and rib cage.

"You good?" He studied her. His gaze raked her from head to toe. Too close. Too aware. Did he see the cracks breaking through her resolve? Or that she was on the verge of falling apart altogether? "Tell me what you need."

She fought for her next inhale, forcing a smile. Need? She needed this case to be over. She needed to collapse into bed for the next several days and sleep. She needed a shower and food and water that hadn't been cleaned by filtration tablets. She needed pain reliever for the aches in her body. All of it combined to tear her down to nothing, and she hated how…weak it made her feel. Useless. Her ex didn't have to be standing right here to tell her how pathetic and needy she was being. His voice had adapted into something familiar and terrifying, her own mental critic. But worst of all? She needed Elias right there with her through whatever came next. Which she hated most of all. "Nothing a bed and a hot meal can't fix."

He considered her for a moment, and she was ready for him to call bullshit. To read her thoughts on her face as he had so many times before. "You're still thinking about that turkey, aren't you?"

She couldn't stop her laugh.

"I can't stop. My mouth is still watering." Sayles didn't wait for his response, turning back to the trail. She didn't know what they would be facing up ahead. She just hoped she'd be enough.

Chapter Twenty-Two

Something was off.

Sayles forged ahead along the rim of the canyon, that impenetrable mask back in place, a few feet ahead. His feet ached. The blisters along the inside of his thigh screamed for new dressings as the weight of his gear wore him down. He'd lost his usual gait in the days they'd pushed themselves to the brink, overcompensating on his right foot and aggravating both injuries. It was harder to breathe up here. Took more effort to take that next step. None of it explained the change in his partner.

She'd lied to him. He'd read it in her face, but Elias wouldn't push. Not yet. Not while they were still on the verge of losing the Hitchhiker Killer to the backcountry spread out ahead. She was on the cusp of burning out. He could already see her instinct to shut down, shut him out, but they'd been through too much already. He couldn't lose any part of her, and that scared him the most. How thoroughly she'd pulled him in with that gut-wrenching smile, borderline rude retorts and sour attitude. How utterly dependent he'd become on her out here. And how quickly he'd given up on making up for his mistakes, for letting his dad down. Justice had always called to him, but with Sayles… It didn't have quite the same pull anymore.

The ground shifted underneath one boot, and Elias jerked to the right. To the edge of the goat trail. His arms went wide in a fight for balance, but he'd overcorrected. A hand shot out to stabilize him—strong and sure—pulling him back to safety. Her fingers dug into his wrist, and his pulse jumped against her touch. Out of control. Then again, when had he been in control around her? His heart had taken a beating over the past two days. Level for one moment and rocketing into the atmosphere the next. He wouldn't be surprised if he failed his next annual physical with the damage he'd done to his cardiovascular system. Not to mention the invisible scars. "Thanks."

A flush worked up her neck, her mouth parting on a strong exhale. "You're not getting out of here that easy."

"Wouldn't dream of it." While he had no intentions of hiking this particular trail again, Elias had already accepted that Zion National Park would be in his future. As many times as it took before she realized he wasn't her bastard of an ex. That she mattered. "You can let go now."

"What?" Sayles dropped her gaze to where her hand gripped his, then pulled away as if he'd burned her. Stepping back, she added a couple feet between them, but no more. Ready to grab him again, he imagined. "Sorry."

He managed not to go tumbling over the edge this time and closed the distance she'd added. Sliding his fingers into her ponytail, Elias tipped her head back, forced her to look up at him. An entire galaxy swirled in her green gaze as dark as any pine tree he'd caught on the way into the park, full of a combination of hesitation and brightness. "I'm not. That's the second time you've saved my life."

"It's a wonder you've gotten this far in life without me."

Her hand found its way to his chest, to push him away or draw him closer, he wasn't sure yet. He didn't dare ask.

His smile tugged at the dry patches at the corners of his mouth. Damn, he hadn't expected this. Hadn't expected her. This case was supposed to be the next rung to getting his career back on track, but she'd solely knocked him down a couple of pegs. "What else does that mouth of yours do?"

"Probably hurt your feelings." There wasn't an inch of give in her position. No inclination to run. Or hide. She stood toe-to-toe, every inch his equal, and he couldn't get enough of the sight. Of the power she held over him.

He couldn't stop the laugh charging through his chest. Releasing his hold on her hair, Elias swiped at the dryness around his mouth. "Go out with me. After this case is finished and I've arrested this asshole we're hunting, go out with me."

"I've slept in your sleeping bag the past two nights, whether I realized it or not." Sayles swung around to face the goat trail, giving him her back. "Kind of feels like we've already missed our chance at a first date."

She wasn't going to make this easy, was she? And, hell, Elias wasn't sure what he would do if she had. He followed in her mud-stiff tracks. "All right. Then tell me what you see happening between us after this case is finished."

Sayles didn't answer for a breath. Two. And he realized he'd stopped breathing to avoid missing her answer. "Why can't we just appreciate what we have now?"

The sucker punch struck as a physical hit that nearly made him falter. "What does that mean?"

Turning her face toward the sun, she gripped her pack's straps. "It means I've lived through the mind games and the manipulation, the isolation and control, and come out on the other side worse for wear. I want to be able to make my own decisions and have a say in my life. For the first time in over a decade, I'm putting myself first, and I'm not sure going from one bad relationship into another is going to give me that freedom."

His hand found hers, and Elias pulled her to a stop. While they were headed for the same end point on this trail—aligned in their goals on this investigation—she'd donned those damn defenses again. He scanned her expression, looking for a way through, but she'd locked him out. "Have I given you any reason to believe I would try to control you like that?"

That intense gaze, highlighted by the sun's arc through the sky, bounced between his eyes. Her lips pursed at the edges. He could see the gutting response forming, but a rush of defeat smoothed her features. "Being thrown together on a death-defying assignment for a couple days doesn't amount to anything, Elias. I knew my ex for years before I married him. There weren't any red flags until it was too late, and I paid for it with eight months behind bars. I refuse to go into anything that blindly."

"You're serious." His fingers tingled to touch her. To pull her against him and remind her she had more instinct than she gave herself credit for. That she was the one who held all the power in this dynamic they'd forged over the course of the investigation. What would it take for her to see herself the way he saw her? "I'm not your ex, Sayles."

"I know that." She slipped her hand out of his, leaving him colder than he'd expected. "That's what makes this all the more terrifying."

Because for her it would be better to go back to that

familiar misery than take a risk on something new. Tension radiated down his spine as he squared off with the meaning behind her words, and it wasn't until right then Elias realized how much he'd allowed himself to hope. For this. For her.

At some point since losing his father, he'd stopped working for anything other than justice. The next killer, the next victim, the next break in the case—they were all that mattered. He'd sacrificed friendships and what little family he'd had left. Nights out, vacations, sick days. Every waking minute had been filled with that unending craving for forgiveness. For not finding the people who'd killed his father, for costing his confidential informant her life. He'd thrown himself into the work until it'd consumed him and left nothing but a husk of the man he'd wanted to be in honor of his father.

Until her.

Over the course of the past two days, he'd felt like a new man. A better man. One who wasn't held back by everything bad that had ever happened to him. None of it had mattered. Because of her. She'd pulled on some internal string he hadn't known existed, hidden deep and out of reach, and had managed to unravel him in a matter of days. He'd had a lot of firsts, but Sayles was the first person to show him he was more than a man shaped by mistakes. That he could be anything he wanted if he just let himself, but that required letting go of that familiar misery, didn't it? He hadn't been prepared for the force of this attraction, and now it was going to cost him. Elias cleared his throat. A distraction. He needed a distraction. Mountains towering over 5,000 feet in elevation crowded around their position along the Narrows cliffs. No way to discern if the Hitchhiker Killer had come this way. "What are the chances the killer will take one of these smaller branches off the end of the trail to avoid us?"

"I don't know. Most of the smaller canyons are impassable after a few hundred feet, which is why park rangers made Big Spring the official end of the trail." Confusion deepened the lines between her brows, but she didn't call him out on the change of subject. "I think he's more likely to head into the backcountry along the east river that feeds into the Narrows. Hikers are required to apply for permits so we can keep track of who is out here and how many, but I doubt he filled out the paperwork. That would make finding him too easy."

"Then we head for the backcountry." Swiping the disappointment to the back of his mind where he would never unpack it again, Elias maneuvered ahead, taking the lead. "Can we access the east river from this trail—"

An explosion of pain ripped through his shoulder.

Sayles's scream echoed off the opposite canyon wall and seared into his brain as he fell back against her. They slammed into the rock face together, his feet hanging over the edge of the trail. Her breath crushed out of her beneath his weight. Long fingers clamped directly over the new hole he'd acquired, and Elias kicked against the dirt to make them as small as a target as possible. They were cornered. Unable to flee without putting them back in the shooter's path. "Stay down."

"You're bleeding." She scrambled to free herself of her pack's straps, but the movement only jarred the bullet lodged in his shoulder deeper.

Elias gritted against the pain.

"That's what happens when you get shot." Her heart

thudded hard against her chest and down his spine. Out of control. Though she wouldn't admit it. Damn it. He had to get them out of here, but short of crawling on their hands and knees, the killer had every advantage. Where was the son of a bitch? He scanned their surroundings. He'd done this, let his personal agenda get in the way of this case. He'd made another mistake. "You need to run. Get out of here. I'll draw him off."

Sayles ripped the top of her pack open, the zipper protesting as she searched for something inside. In a matter of breaths, the first aid kit was balanced on her knee, and she popped the lid. "I'm not leaving you here to fight him alone. We barely survived the last time. We have better odds together."

"Well, isn't that romantic." The Hitchhiker Killer blocked the path ahead. Raising his weapon. And took aim at Sayles. "I hope I'm not interrupting, but as I said before I do have need of your assistance, Ranger Green, and I'm on a bit of a schedule." He motioned Sayles up with the wave of the gun. "So, if you don't mind, chop chop."

Positioning himself in front of her, Elias set himself up as a shield. Though he wasn't sure it would do a damn bit of good considering he already had two holes punctured in his torso. Her hands clamped over the wound in his shoulder. Even at gunpoint, she was trying to ensure he wouldn't bleed out in front of her. "She's not going anywhere with you."

Elias didn't give the bastard the chance to pull the trigger. He lunged. The collision knocked him off-balance.

With a single shove, Elias went over the cliff.

Chapter Twenty-Three

"No!" She dived for the spot where Elias had disappeared.

The ground rushed to meet her in a frenzy of dirt and lacerating gravel. Her chest threatened to cave under the impact as she reached for nothing but air.

He was gone. There one second and gone the next. Acidic loss burned up her throat. No. It wasn't possible. This was all some kind of nightmare. She was going to wake up. Any minute now they'd be in her one-person tent, her sprawled across his chest and him acting like he'd gotten the best night sleep of his life. They would have breakfast together and throw barbs at each other. He would flash her that smile that went straight to her insides and maybe kiss her again. "Elias!"

Only the Virgin River's roar answered. Tears burned in her eyes.

"Yes, very sad. Shall we go?" A strong hand wrapped around her biceps and hauled her to her feet. Her legs had turned to Jell-O. Her inability to get her feet underneath her—to comply—testified to his strength as an all-around psychopath. "As I said, I'm on a deadline, and I've already wasted enough time trying to get my hands on you for this little project."

They were moving. Along the trail. Away from where

Elias had gone over the edge. She couldn't just leave him. There was still a chance he'd survived, right? Sayles ripped her arm out the killer's grasp. "I'm not going anywhere with you."

Stumbling back, she spun on her heel. Ready to launch down the trail. But she didn't make it far. She saw his shadow first. Then came the pain. Crushing weight tackled her into the ground. Her knee slipped over the edge of the two-foot-wide goat trail, but the killer's weight held her in place. Her forehead bounced off slick mud. White explosions danced behind her eyes. Air. She couldn't breathe. Excruciating agony threatened to snap her spine in half as she tried to suck in a breath.

"Unfortunately, Ranger Green, that's not your decision." He fisted his hand in her hair and pulled, forcing her back to compensate. The barrel of his gun cut into the side of her face. Somehow warm and cold at the same time. Mouth pressed against her ear, he exerted pure dominance over her. "Now, I've been patient up until now. Keep fighting me and I will burn this entire park to the ground before throwing you into the flames. Do you understand?"

The grip on her scalp tightened. Tears leaked from the corners of her eyes, quickly dying with the gust of wind over the top of the canyon. Not from the pain but the sudden gulf of darkness bleeding from her heart. Right where Elias had set up residence. She'd convinced herself she'd known emptiness and loss, but it was nothing compared to the void chipping away at her now. Dirt infiltrated her mouth and nose; thick layers of mud stuck to her uniform and face.

"Say the words." Another wave of pain punctuated

the Hitchhiker Killer's point. "Say that you understand what's at stake."

Every cell in her body fought against agreeing to anything this man wanted. The fight might physically cost her, but inside, she knew Elias would expect nothing less. Her teeth locked. "Go to hell."

"Oh, Ranger Green, where do you think I came from?" The pressure against her spine vanished.

She managed to suck in a lungful of oxygen a split second before the killer wrenched her upward by her hair. Slapping both hands over his to ease the pain, she had little physical control facing him. Any second now, Elias would drag himself over the lip of the canyon. He would tell this bastard to let her go. He'd look like hell but throw her that crooked smile to ease the anxiety churning nausea in her gut. One second. Two. She waited. Ignored the Hitchhiker Killer's prompts for her attention. And waited. The hard pound of her heartbeat between her ears stretched seconds into minutes, into what felt like hours. But he never came, and her heart broke all over again. Gone. He was gone.

He'd been right there for the past two days. At her side. Keeping her from mentally breaking when all she'd wanted to do was curl into a ball and disappear. Elias had seen through the armor she'd built around herself and accepted every broken piece she'd tried to hide from the outside world, and she'd thrown it back in his face. Unwilling to give up a sliver of the hurt she'd survived in favor of the unknown. Because she'd been scared. Unfairly compared him to her ex when they couldn't be more different. She'd regret it for the rest of her life.

"Let's go, and if you try anything like that little rock-in-your-bag maneuver, I will shoot you in the arm. Then the other arm. And then I'll move on to your hands until there is nothing left of you." The killer shoved her forward, and it took everything in her not to hit the ground a second time. He collected her pack and tossed it at her chest with too much force. "You won't need them where we're going."

She faced off with golden-yellow sun making its way toward the horizon, brushing off layers of dirt from her uniform shirt. Sweat beaded at her temples despite the consistent breeze skirting the rim of the canyon. "Asshole."

His laugh hit wrong, disingenuous and sickly. He didn't answer, but she had a feeling he wasn't the first person people invited over to dinner.

"Where are we going?" Sayles kept awareness at her back while searching for a way to escape. Rocks shifted beneath her boots, the gravel much looser here than along other parts of the trail as they closed in on Big Spring. She could throw a handful in his face. Give herself a head start, but she wasn't sure her ribs could hold up against another tackle. Emerald-colored waters rippled 1,000 feet below under the onslaught of two medium-size waterfalls. The river was shallowest here, a hub that swelled only with the onslaught of storms. There was no surviving a jump from this distance. Elias had fallen at a deeper section. He could've survived. He could need help.

"If I told you that, I'd be ruining the surprise. All you need to worry about is helping me avoid any other ranger patrols." The killer's footsteps kept in time with hers. Deliberate. Intimidating. He wanted her to know he could strike out, that he was the one in control here.

Damn it. Why had Elias put himself between her and the man at her back? He had to have known he'd lose a fight against a gun, but he'd made the choice to protect her anyway. To give her a chance to run. Because that was the kind of man he was. A protector, through and through, with the weight of the entire world on his shoulders. No one else would've been good enough to do the job, but that relentlessness had forced him to sacrifice so much. And for a stupid minute, she'd convinced herself she could be the one to help him break free of those self-inflicted responsibilities. For a stupid minute, she'd considered saying yes. But handing her heart over to someone else—giving him the same power she'd granted her ex—scared her more than falling over the edge of this cliff. She couldn't do that. She couldn't go through that again,

Sayles glanced back, vying for a view of the river. For some sign Elias wasn't dead.

"I've never met someone who thinks so loudly before." A nudge in her lower spine forced her to look ahead. The gun took shape in her peripheral vision. "Whatever escape you're considering, Ranger Green, it won't work. I will find you, and you will wish you were dead."

She was out of options. No weapon. No escape from this trail. Her best chance was to get them to the back-country and wait for the opportunity to run where she didn't have to fight the elevation, a too-narrow trail or the river itself. But biding her time could cost Elias precious minutes he didn't have. "What do you want from me?"

"Keep moving. Daylight's burning." Coldness—all too familiar and terrifying—solidified the killer's face as he guided her forward, and Sayles couldn't help but conclude this was going to end badly. For her. For Elias. For anyone else who came across this man's path.

She was the only one standing in his way of him getting what he wanted. Whatever that was.

They kept to the goat trail, bypassing the beauty of Big Spring below. This was the official end of the Narrows. That emerald pool below had changed her every time she'd hiked this trail. In small ways at first, then with life-altering clarity. Zion National Park held a magic to it she couldn't explain, one of possibility and healing and support. But she didn't feel it now. People liked to think time healed all wounds, but those people were idiots. Wounds like hers didn't heal. She'd just had to learn how to control the bleeding.

Gravel crunched under her weight as they hiked past the oasis 1,000 feet, down then shifted to fine-grained dirt and sand. Desert weeds clawed at her shins and caught on her bootlaces as they entered backcountry. Waves of mountains crested and dipped against the crystal-blue sky. The rock here took on more of a pale tan coloring compared with the red and orange along the Narrows, but it was still just as beautiful. Miles of unending desert, canyon and green trees stretched out before them, but Sayles didn't have the guts to stop to take it all in this time.

"Northeast." One word. That was all he gave her as they approached a lightning-struck tree, its black bark smooth where animals and weather had worn it down over the years.

Shards of wood warned her not to get too close, and she couldn't help compare herself to those broken pieces. Sharp. Burned. Exposed. At first glance, she would've assumed the tree had reached the end of its life, as she had. Under arrest for a murder she hadn't committed, imprisoned with no sign of release, captive by a man who'd promised her the world. She and this tree had a lot in common. Except, as the Hitchhiker Killer nudged her a second time, she caught sight of new growth. Dead center in the middle of the charred remains of the tree. Surrounded by all the bad, a wisp of life.

She'd had that these past couple of days. A glimpse of something alive and renewing. Made possible by the federal agent she was so determined to hate. Her past had lost its grip in his laugh, in the way he'd put her needs first. How he'd risked his life for hers. No one had done that before. Sayles slowed her descent down the rounded, cracked hill leading into unfamiliar territory of Zion's backcountry. No one was likely to do what he had for her again, and she'd wasted it. By letting fear win. By not telling Elias how he'd changed her, gifted her something no one else had. How he'd gotten her to dream again.

Unsure how long they traversed the desert in silence, Sayles was caught off guard by the bright spot of blue against the natural landscaping a few hundred yards ahead. Her heart shot into her throat. Hikers. Her skin turned clammy as she checked to see if the killer had noticed. The park was supposed to be evacuated, but it was impossible to hunt down every visitor in a short amount of time, especially those who came to the park to get off the grid. She made no assumptions that she'd make it out of this alive, but she could still save innocent bystanders.

She cut to the left, leading the Hitchhiker Killer more northeast. Hoping to bypass the tent altogether without drawing attention to it. But it was too late.

"It'd be awfully rude of us if we didn't say hello." Patrick dragged her back in front of him, the barrel of his weapon pressed into her ribs, and led her straight for the low voices coming from inside the blue canvas. "Don't you think?"

Chapter Twenty-Four

He was dead.

That was the only explanation for the white light taking up his vision.

Elias blinked to get a better sense of his surroundings. Walls of red, orange and green bled through the brightness and took shape in his peripheral vision. Was dying supposed to hurt this much? Hell. Every inch of his body screamed. Dragging his chin to his chest, he mentally cataloged which of his limbs worked and which he'd have to let go of. Where was the train that had hit him? Water beat against one side of his face and seeped past his lips. Gross.

Turning onto his side, he let the groan stuck in his throat free. Rock cut into his hip and rib cage. Damn it. That hurt. He pressed his hand to his side to somehow keep himself together. A barrage of memory slapped into place. The killer. The cliff. The fall. Holy hell. He'd gone over the edge. And survived. That had to qualify for the Guinness World Records. He craned his head up, where he imagined the spot from which he'd done a Peter Pan into the river below, but he was too far away to tell.

Elias struggled to get his feet under him, moving slower than he wanted to. A scream echoed through his head and sent his heart rate into overdrive. Sayles. She'd tried to grab on to him. She was still up there. Alone with a killer who wouldn't let her walk away unscathed. He had to move. If he started the climb now, he might reach the goat trail by sundown. Searching the top of the rock wall, he failed to see any sort of movement.

Moving his arm, he noted blood on his shirt. His abdominal wound had reopened. The fall must've torn it open. He'd lost his pack. His first aid kit. Sayles. There would be no cleaning or bandaging it this time. He stumbled as he straightened. Not good. "Damn."

The hydro bib's straps dug into his shoulders; his gear was full of water. It would only work to slow him down. Hauling himself to the edge of the river, he surveyed his current location. Oversize stair steps jutted out from the base of the canyon, overgrown with trees and shrubs. Okay. Not one of the corridors. He had to be close to the end of the trail then, to Big Spring. Elias cleared the river, collapsing on a rock lip double his height. He unlaced his boots and dumped water from each. The blisters would be a bitch with wet socks, but he didn't have time for his gear to dry. Sayles needed him now. Discarding the hydro bib, he left it behind as he scanned the canyon walls.

They'd accessed the goat trail around the four-mile marker. If the river had swept him downstream, he should be close enough to get back on. Except this time he wouldn't have any gear, he had a hole in his torso and the sun would give out in the next hour or so. Who wouldn't bet on him? Elias kept to the edge of the river, careful of every slippery, algae-covered rock threatening to bring him down. If he was being honest with himself, he might not get back up.

Attempting to hold his blood inside his body, he navigated the trail downstream. Every cell in his body begged him to give up now. To wait until Grant or another ranger could lead the manhunt, but Sayles didn't have that kind of time. And he wasn't going to be another person in her life to give up as her friends and family had when she'd gone to prison.

She deserved better. Deserved to be happy after everything she'd survived. Not just her emotionally abusive husband but the grief and loneliness that came with betrayal. But she couldn't see it. How ridiculously beautiful and strong she'd become in response to her circumstances. And his heart hurt at seeing her continually retreat into that shell of a survivor she'd come to rely on since her arrest. Because he'd been privileged enough to glimpse through that armor, to the woman underneath. The one who took risks in moving to a whole new state to find a new path, who put her life on the line for tourists and hikers every day, who gifted a nobody like him with new purpose. Showed him how to stop letting the bad things win. In a matter of days, she'd changed him. Reached deep into his soul and resurrected a piece of himself he hadn't realized he'd let die with every failed date and case gone wrong. She'd brought him back to life.

So, no. He wasn't giving up on her. He'd keep going until the killer finished the job, or Sayles told him to go to hell. Either way, he owed her that much.

Elias left the cold dependence of the river and braced himself to ascend the goat trail a second time. His legs protested each step, but he had to keep moving. He already carried the weight of one innocent life on his shoulder. He wasn't sure he could support another. Gravel shifted beneath his boots, and he had to use more of his upper body to stay balanced. Step after step, shallow breath after shallow breath. The pain in his side speared throughout the rest of his torso, as if a nerve ending had been struck.

He was going to make it. Because there wasn't any other option.

Sun penetrated his vision, blinding him and gold-washing the landscape ahead as he crested the lip of the canyon. Hand up to block the sun, Elias picked up the pace into a reckless jog. The pressure in his chest hadn't let up from the moment he'd gained consciousness on that canyon floor. Whatever plans the Hitchhiker Killer had for Sayles, it didn't include letting her walk away. Her clock had started the moment he'd gone over the edge of the trail, but he wouldn't leave her to fight this alone.

His lungs burned. From the elevation, exertion or dropping temperatures, he didn't know, and it sure as hell wasn't going to slow him down. Shallow footprints took shape in front of him, one set smaller than the others. Sayles. She'd been here. He was getting close. "Come on."

Utter exhaustion clawed beneath his skin, and a gush of blood filled his palm as he added pressure to the wound. The two were probably linked, but logic wasn't running this show. He was racing against the clock on pure need. Need to get to Sayles, to catch this killer, to make his father proud. All of it combined in a heavy dose of adrenaline that wouldn't last long if he pushed too hard. But what other choice did he have?

The trail flattened out in front of him. Mountains demanded attention from every angle with valleys hidden by an insurmountable amount of trees and brush. Sayles could be anywhere, and without her as a guide, all he could do was trust his instincts. "This isn't going to end well."

Elias stepped off the goat trail and into the unknown. Sweat won the battle against the sun, seeping through his T-shirt despite the onslaught of drying heat. His ankles ached from uneven terrain, but he'd just add it to the long list of problems he'd have to deal with later. If he survived. Patches of snow highlighted the northern peaks of the cliffs staring down at him as he cut his own route into the first valley. Gravity added to the weight on his body, and it took everything he had left not to fall face-first into the dirt.

No signs of life. Of anyone else out here. The killer had to have brought her this way. There were no other branches to follow at the end of the Narrows, but the park itself stretched over two hundred square miles. A gust cut through the valley and whipped up the dirt under his feet, erasing any kind of tracks. Still, Elias's gut told him he was headed in the right direction, as if Sayles had connected that invisible internal string she'd discovered inside him to herself. To give him something to focus on. To follow.

And, hell, he'd follow her to the ends of the earth. He'd chase her forever if that was what she required of him, to show her she was worth every second, every mistake, everything he'd be required to give up for a single shot with her.

There were no paths out here in the backcountry, but he kept heading forward. Blood crusted in his palm and between his fingers though the pain remained consistent. Pulsing and unrelenting. It was too late to go back now. Backup wouldn't get here in time. Without Sayles, he was stranded in the middle of the desert without any idea where to go next, food, medical supplies or a way to contact the visitors' center. All he could hope for was that Grant had gotten enough information on their location to provide support, whatever that looked like.

He was on his own, but this was what he'd trained for. What he was good at. He'd studied the thinking patterns and motivations of killers for years, including the very people involved in his father's death. The Hitchhiker Killer wouldn't be any different. There was a reason he'd followed the interstate to Zion National Park. Elias had originally assumed it'd been to avoid arrest, but most criminals wouldn't trade a nine-by-nine cell and three meals a day for an early death in the middle of the desert. The closest thing to civilization outside the park was Springdale, a tourist town constructed and dependent on the lure of the park, but the town sat completely in the opposite direction. No. The killer wasn't looking to escape. Sayles had said he was looking for something. Someone. But who the hell would be out here?

The answer came as Elias rounded the next bend in the unofficial trail. In the form of a blue canvas tent. The entrance had been left unzipped, the makeshift door collapsing into the tent and exposing the window at the back. A white-and-red cooler lay discarded on its side, melted ice leaking into the dirt in a spreading dark patch.

More evidence of a struggle peppered the dead landscape. A paperback—tossed face down into the dirt—a shredded sleeping bag thrown over a cactus a few feet away.

And the foot peeking out from the corner of the tent.

Dread pooled at the base of his spine, pulling Elias to a stop. He studied the boot-clad foot, willed it to move. Compared it to the pair Sayles had been wearing these past two days, and the dread turned into something darker as he recognized the brand. No. No, no, no. It wasn't her. It couldn't be her. Then he was running. "Sayles."

Dirt kicked up under his shoes as he rounded the tent. And froze.

Chest heaving, wound bleeding, Elias studied the body, doubling over. Nausea churned in his gut, and he had to look away as horse flies started circling. He'd faced bodies before, but this one…

Not Sayles. The face he studied belonged to that of a stranger. Hispanic male dressed in a denim button-up shirt and shorts, full mustache with a peppering of beard growth. Maybe thirty, thirty-five years old. The park was supposed to be evacuated. What was he doing out here by himself? Blood clotted around the bullet wound between the victim's eyes. Fresh. Couldn't have been shot more than thirty minutes ago, which meant he still had a chance of catching up.

National park rangers would have to collect the body. For now, Elias grabbed a half-eaten bag of beef jerky, shoved a handful into his mouth and searched through the tent for something—anything—to help him find Sayles. No radio. No weapons. He tossed a second sleeping bag to the other side of the tent. And realized this victim hadn't been out here alone after all.

The Hitchhiker Killer had taken another hostage.

Chapter Twenty-Five

A scream seared her nervous system.

Not hers. Though Sayles was close to losing her mind as images of a bullet ripping through that man's head refused to dissipate. She'd been forced to leave him there next to his tent, his pleas for his wife's life still shredding through her.

But it'd just been a game. One the killer had already decided the winner. Empty promises of choosing one victim while the other would walk away unscathed replayed through her head as she'd just stood there, trying to make herself as small as possible so as not to regain the Hitchhiker Killer's attention. Except Patrick had never intended to let either of the campers go. Instead, he'd pulled the trigger and left an innocent man die at her feet. There hadn't been anything she could've done to stop him. Not without taking a bullet herself.

She stumbled forward as the toe of her boot caught on a rock and turned to see that gun still aimed at her back even as the man dragged the female camper across the desert floor by her pretty blond hair. Sayles didn't know where they were going, had no idea how to get out of this mess. They were at the mercy of a man who possessed no mercy. This… She wasn't trained for this. What happened now? "Please, you don't have to hurt her."

Another scream bounced off the mountains around them as the killer wrenched the woman's head back, and Sayles's heart squeezed too hard in her chest. The camper had dropped to her knees, trying to keep up with the killer's push forward. Dirt-crusted blood trickled down her shins and pooled along the tops of her white socks. "You're right. I don't have to hurt her, but it's been a long time coming. You deserve what's coming, don't you, Mae?"

Mae.

Shock slapped Sayles across the face with an invisible hand. Her legs threatened to collapsed right out from under her. How… How did he know her name? The hairs on the back of Sayles's neck stood on end, and she wanted nothing but to escape. Run as fast as she could and never look back as realization set in. She tried to pick up on details of the woman's face, to give herself something to keep her grounded. The soft curve of groomed eyebrows, the way her flannel shirt—much too big for her frame—hung off her shoulders and revealed the tank top underneath. None of it did a damn bit of good. "You… you know her?"

"Mae and I go a long way back, don't we?" The killer smoothed the pad of his thumb along the woman's cheek. "Years, in fact."

Tears streaked down the camper's—down Mae's—face as she latched both hands on to the killer's wrist for relief. But there was no escape as long as Patrick kept that gun on them. Sayles could try to run, but that would leave this woman, whoever she was, in the hands of a man who looked as though he was one wrong response away from putting a bullet in both of them. The sobs intensified, each striking Sayles harder than the one before. "He's my... He was my husband."

The world almost tipped on its axis. Sayles tried to focus on something—anything—but the cavern tearing through her chest.

"*Was?* Are you kidding me, Mae?" The Hitchhiker Killer tugged Mae's head back against his abdomen with more force than necessary, earning a whimper that Sayles found all too familiar. She'd heard it before, coming from her own mouth as her ex stood above her screaming for an answer as to why she hadn't picked up the phone when he'd called. "I seem to recall you telling me it was death do us part. So, no, Ranger Green. I was not her husband. I *am* her husband, and it's time for Mae to come home."

The control, the domination and manipulation—it was all coming back in full force. Unfiltered terror surfaced. Sweat broke across her skin despite the dip of the sun behind the mountain to the west. The urge to shrink, to hide, wrestled with the new facets she'd forged since her release from prison. The ones that told her she was stronger than her abuser, that she'd survived, that she'd won. They felt like nothing more than the sand stuck between her fingers compared to the black hole dragging at her body, anything but solid.

She couldn't let it win. Couldn't let this man win. She'd stood up to this particular killer before, shown him she wouldn't be beaten down to that husk of a woman again. It hadn't been a conscious effort but created from choice. From Elias showing her exactly how much power she exerted. Her choice. It'd always been her choice when it came to him, and…and she loved him for it.

The solid wall of adamant she'd built between her and the rest of the world had crumbled in a matter of days because of him. Because he'd encouraged her to trust herself, to save herself while he'd stood nearby in case she needed help. And she'd used that agency to reject the idea there could ever be anything between them. She'd been wrong. So wrong. What she wouldn't give to wake up pressed against Elias's chest in a too-small tent again. To hear that laugh that physically brushed her insides and surged heat into her face. To feel his mouth on hers and forget all the hurt and the pain and the bitterness.

She'd started falling for him. And lost the chance to tell him.

Trusting Elias with her heart wasn't about giving up her freedom. He'd never take that from her. He'd never cage or isolate her as her ex had. It was about choosing him over that deep-rooted fear. And she wanted to choose him. More than anything. Regret fought to consume her whole, but she wouldn't give it leverage.

Squeezing her pack to her chest, Sayles understood in that moment what she had to do, what she wished someone else had done for her. She took that initial step to close the distance between her and Patrick, with Mae positioned between them.

Mae's cries shook through her. Blond hair fisted around the killer's hand, she couldn't budge an inch without his permission and the Hitchhiker Killer wasn't about to let her go again. Sayles could read it in the deadpan expression etched into his face. "How…how did you find me?"

"You didn't think I would let my favorite plaything off

the leash without having a tracker to keep tabs on you, did you? It took some bribing, but your dentist left a few thousand dollars richer during your last cleaning. Unfortunately for him, he didn't live long enough to spend it." Zero remorse laced his words. As if violating his ex-wife had become an everyday occurrence, and Sayles had no doubt of the depths of his depravity to claim something that didn't belong to him. The killer hauled Mae up by her hair, pressing his mouth to her ear. "Time to go home, darling. Where you belong."

"Please, Patrick. Don't do this." Sayles took another step, grabbing on to that smallest bit of confidence Elias had praised her for so many times and holding on tight. The second the Hitchhiker Killer got his ex out of the park, Mae's chances of survival plummeted. She couldn't let that happen. Not now. Not ever again. "I can help you. Nobody has to get hurt."

"I'm not your wife anymore." Mae shook her head, seemingly running out of tears. She was losing energy. Burning through whatever remnants of adrenaline her body had produced upon seeing her partner killed in front of her, and Sayles needed her to keep fighting. "I left. I'm happy. Javier—"

"Is dead, Mae. What did you think would happen?" The killer stabbed the barrel of the gun into his ex-wife's temple, his index finger over the trigger. Her silent scream told Sayles how much pain he'd inflicted, that he wanted it to hurt. "That I would just let another man put his hands on you? Kiss you? Take you to bed and not pay for touching you?"

"Please." Defeat and grief battled across Mae's freckled face as she struggled to get free of her ex, and Sayles couldn't wait anymore.

"Please, what?" Patrick pressed his face against Mae's tears. "Let you go? I gave you everything. A house, a better life. I paid for your clothes, your food, anything you wanted. All I wanted in return was for you to love me as much as I loved you, but you just couldn't do that, could you?"

"You killed him." Mae was on the verge of losing herself to the anger, the grief.

Now. Sayles had to go now. "Hey, Patrick?"

His gaze locked on hers.

"Go to hell." Sayles threw her pack at the killer as hard she could. The weight slammed against his chest and knocked him back. The gun arced away from Mae's head. Just for a moment. Sayles grabbed for the woman's hand and tugged, forcing Mae to her feet. "Run!"

The desert stretched out in front of them.

The gun exploded from behind, and Sayles's instinct automatically had her ducking her head to avoid a bullet. She clutched on to Mae as hard as she dared so they wouldn't be separated, blocking her head with her other hand. As if it would be enough to stop dying as Javier had. "Come on!"

The last slivers of watery sunlight vanished from the horizon, leaving nothing but a warm orange glow in the sky. Within minutes, they'd have nothing but their pathetic human vision to navigate the wilderness, but it was enough. It would have to be enough. Weeds and cacti clawed at their exposed shins as they worked together to create as much distance between them and Patrick as possible.

"Mae!" Rage coated that one word, hiking Sayles's defenses into overdrive. A second gunshot ripped through the night, but they couldn't stop. Not yet. Not yet. "I will find you, Mae! I will make you pay for those ninety-two days you've been gone."

The air was thinner here at 5,500 feet. Dizziness swam through her head, but she only dragged Mae to her side, unwilling to let go as they confronted the base of the mountain to the east. Her boots caught on a rock she hadn't detected with her adjusting vision, and Sayles hit the ground. Cactus needles pierced the skin of her palms, and it took everything she had not to scream in pain. To give away their position.

"Are you okay?" Mae tried to help her to her feet.

"Keep going." Scanning the massive wall of rock in front of them, Sayles ignored the agony in her chest and knees. She'd hit harder than she expected, but it wasn't enough to stop her from escaping. "We have to climb."

The mountain seemed to ignore their desperation, throwing obstacles in their path as they clawed upward. Patches of rock and weeds bled together in the lack of sunlight. Snakes and scorpions—along with much more dangerous wildlife—lived in these mountains, but Sayles couldn't think about any of them right now.

"You can't hide from me! I will find you both, and when I do I'll finish this, I swear. You'll never leave me again, Mae." Patrick's voice had gained some distance. "Shall we play a game of Marco Polo? Marco…"

Sayles's hand flattened on a length of rock that went deeper into the mountain. Cool air brushed across her face, almost begging her to get closer. She shoved Mae ahead of her, keeping her voice low. "In here."

"Marco!" That single word tensed the muscles down Sayles's spine.

The cave mouth wasn't large, but it would provide them a couple minutes of rest. That was all they could afford. Sayles scrambled across the dirt-covered floor, maneuvering Mae deeper, away from the entrance. A burning odor clogged the back of her throat, but they had no other choice.

"Behind me." She positioned Mae at her back as she faced off with the mouth of the cave. A shadow crossed at the entrance, and Sayles fought down a shiver.

His frame came into view, dark against the backdrop of the last glow of the day. "Marco…"

Chapter Twenty-Six

The sound of the gunshot drilled straight through him.

Elias picked up the pace, following the curve of the mountain. He was losing blood, losing energy, but every step got him that much closer to Sayles and whoever else the killer had taken hostage. It was harder to breathe now. If he hadn't been scheduled for a heart attack anytime soon, this manhunt would do the trick.

Forcing himself to slow, he tried to pick out evidence of movement or voices. The rustle of wind through scrub was all that responded. All right. He had to think despite his ability to grit through the pain; he was leaking. He wasn't sure how much blood he'd already lost while unconscious in the river, but he had to guess any amount would come back and bite him in the ass if he didn't get a handle on the situation. Damn it. He should've grabbed the campers' first aid kit, but in the moment, all he'd been able to think about was Sayles. Getting to her.

And it was too late to turn back now.

Those gunshots hadn't been for nothing. His partner could be out here hurt or worse. The Hitchhiker Killer would have a hard time controlling two hostages, no matter the circumstances. And he knew Sayles. She would take the first opportunity to escape, but that meant leaving an innocent in the killer's hands, which wouldn't even cross her mind. Even with the threat of death barreling down on her, she'd do whatever it took to protect someone else. It was one of the things he loved about her most, and hell, he wouldn't change it.

He loved her.

All the retorts she threw in his face, her rashness and impulsivity, the way she fought to keep her mouth closed when a thought was on her mind. The ranger advertised every emotion of her face and gave him a front-row seat to the whirlwind of danger flashing in her eyes when he'd gotten too close to a line she'd drawn between them. He loved how she unconsciously sought him out in the middle of the night and that his body melted against her when nothing but exhaustion and sleeping pills had done the trick in the past. He just…loved her.

All the bad dates, all the loneliness, the obsession with his work—he'd go through it all again if it meant he could keep Sayles in his life. He'd even hike the Narrows again if it gifted him with a glimpse of her in her element. Because here, in this park, she'd freed herself, and he couldn't help but be drawn in. To want that for himself. Without him even realizing it, she'd filled the hollow spaces in his chest, highlighting just how empty he'd been without her.

"Where would you go, Ranger Green?" Elias sucked in a deep breath, scanning the barren landscape. He wasn't familiar with these mountains. Well, hell, he wasn't familiar with any portion of this park, but Sayles was. If she had a chance to get away, she would take it, and she would take the second hostage with her. And hide. He'd noted enough half caves and outcroppings in the rock walls of the canyon to know these mountains most likely had similar structure. Okay. She would head for a hiding spot. Wait the killer out until they could escape unnoticed or until help arrived. But they would've had to have moved fast. The Hitchhiker Killer had a gun, after all. He would've gone after them, desperate to keep what he thought he was owed.

Which begged the question, why take a random camper hostage alongside Sayles? Why increase the risk of one or both of them turning on him? Unless the killer had been looking for that specific camper. Sayles thought he might've been searching for someone the killer deemed important. Not something. Someone he knew. What if he'd been engaged in his own hunt? All the murders on the highway, the death of the hiker at the base of the Narrows—it hadn't been random at all. It'd led the Hitchhiker Killer to Zion's backcountry, to that tent and his latest victim.

Surveying the nearest mountain, Elias tried to discern any caves or outcroppings in the rock face, but it was far too dark for his pathetic vision to pick up. He'd have to get closer, risk heading in the wrong direction for the slightest chance of learning Sayles's location. But psychology and the body's automatic fight-or-flight response dictated humans as a whole sought immediate safety when threatened, which meant Sayles had most likely run to the mountain southeast of his position. Once she'd added some distance between her and the killer, she'd try to make her way back to civilization.

Jogging the few hundred yards to the base of the mountain, he sounded like an asthmatic pug. His atoms had started vibrating at dangerously high intensity, threatening to crack him open from the inside out. But he'd push through. Not because of some outdated need for justice but for Sayles. For their future. Because there would be one. He'd make sure of it.

Something solid and out of place took shape on the ground ahead, and Elias slowed his pace. Every sense on alert. The lump wasn't moving. Didn't hold any life. Not a person. A pack. Toeing the material, he flipped it face up. And froze.

Sayles's pack. She'd been here. But worse, a national park ranger had abandoned a mass of supplies she'd guarded more carefully than a dragon and its hoard. She wouldn't have given it up for anything, which meant it'd either been taken from her by the killer or she'd surrendered it to give herself a better chance at survival. Either way, she needed him now. Tipping the pack upside down, he crouched, emptying the contents into the dirt. He hit the power button for the flashlight and slipped the end between his teeth to get a better accounting of what was left. Bingo. The first aid kit. He didn't bother with cleaning the wound in his side this time around, drying the edges with one of her shirts and slapping a new section of gauze to hold him together. He could hear Sayles's criticism in the back of his head now. How she'd argue he was doing more harm than good in leaving the hole to fester. How he'd regret it and probably turn into a brain-craving zombie, but for now, it would be enough to get him to her.

He couldn't control a groan as he got to his feet. Elias braced himself against the mountain's wall, holding his side to keep the new gauze in place. Dirt shifted beneath his boots, and that damn blister between his thighs burned. His vision played tricks on him as stars began peppering the velvet night sky. There one second and gone the next. Or maybe he'd finally started losing his mind. Hard to tell when stranded out in the middle of desert, his drinking water had run out and he'd been surviving off adrenaline fumes for two days straight. "Keep it together, man."

The pep talk didn't hit as hard as he'd intended, but he pushed upward, legs protesting the slightest shift in his balance. Hard-to-see claws caught on his jeans and tore at his exposed arms. Stinging pain ripped at the side of his thigh. Damn cactus. The mountainside had gone from vivid red rock stained with water damage to nothing but a black landscape determined to tear him apart. The moon had yet to make an appearance in the east while the sun had already given up the ghost. He was in the dark. Thoroughly and completely surrounded by nothing but the unknown.

Except he knew Sayles was there. Waiting for him. Pulling him in, and he wouldn't fail her. Not as he'd failed the last innocent life entrusted to him. Trees rustled on either side of him, as if disturbed by something he couldn't see. The ground flattened out under his feet, and his lungs eased up on trying to kill him. Elias nearly fell to his knees as gravity lessened its mission to pull him back down the mountain.

The black hole staring back at him wasn't large by any means. At least nothing compared to the massive echoing caverns he'd explored as a kid. No. This cave hadn't wanted to be discovered, hidden back away from prying eyes, and he couldn't help but shiver at all the possibilities waiting inside. This. This was where Sayles would've taken cover if she'd managed to escape the Hitchhiker

Killer. To buy herself enough time before going for help. Or fighting back.

No signs of life or death. Just a stillness that crept into Elias's bones and waited for him to make the next move. He scanned the stretch of black emptiness behind him, light outlines of mountains and deep valleys bleeding into his vision. Then stepped over the threshold of the cave.

The ceiling dipped down, scratching against his scalp. At over six feet, he had to watch his head. The walls themselves pressed in on him from every angle but led him deeper into the belly of the mountain. His footsteps and skids echoed around him, announcing his presence to anyone inside. Silence—deadly and expansive—took up residence in his head. He arced the flashlight beam toward his feet, careful of every step, with his free hand sliding against rough stone wall caked in dust. "Not creepy at all."

But he'd endure a thousand caves just like this if it meant finding Sayles at the end. He didn't know how they would make it work with him assigned out of Vegas and over state lines, but whatever happened in this park wouldn't be the end of them. Not as long as he had any say about it. He'd been an idiot to think he could come out here and fix his career—to pretend that working cases harder would make him happy, that it could fix the fact that he hadn't caught his father's killers—when all he really needed was a heavy dose of prickly national park ranger to set him straight. She hadn't meant to do it. He knew that. Neither of them had meant for any of this, but that didn't mean they got to turn their backs on it, either. Walk away as though they hadn't been altered on a cellular level just by being in the same proximity as each other.

No. Elias had already lost too much. He wasn't going to lose Sayles, too.

She'd hate that he'd called her prickly, and he couldn't wait to test out his theory.

Elias navigated farther into the mountain. Then heard a voice. No. A whimper.

His rib cage suctioned tighter around his organs. He picked up the pace, pressing his back into the curve of wall ahead. Just beyond a pool of flashlight highlighting his park ranger. She'd taken a defensive stance in front of another woman he didn't recognize. He didn't have a weapon. He had nothing on his side but years of field-work and training burning to be let free at the sight of those women at the hands of a cold-blooded killer. And he'd make every move count. Elias slipped around the corner, closing the distance between him and the Hitch-hiker Killer as quietly as possible.

"There's nowhere you can run that I won't find you." Raising his arm, the killer brandished the gun. Taking aim directly at Sayles's chest. "And you've both tested my patience beyond my usual limits."

Sayles shifted her weight between both feet, keeping the killer's attention locked on her and away from the sob-bing woman clinging at her back.

The killer took a single step forward. "We always knew it would end like this, Ranger Green. Thank you for your help in locating my wife. I couldn't have done it with-out you."

Elias clenched the flashlight under his knuckles. "I think it's safe to say she quits."

Chapter Twenty-Seven

She was either going to have a heart attack or faint.

Sayles couldn't decide.

That voice. She knew that voice. The gravelly undertones urged her to breathe while delivering warning straight to her gut. Elias. He was alive, but she couldn't discern his condition as the federal agent who'd singlehandedly upturned her life lunged.

Mae's fingernails dug into her arms a split second before the impact.

Elias collided with the Hitchhiker Killer. Flashlight beams scattered across the cave walls and blinded her. White lights danced across her vision. She pressed Mae into the dead end they'd reached a few minutes before, completely powerless as the sound of fists and groans and pain ricocheted around them.

"Sayles, go!"

Elias's command shoved her into action. She grabbed for the woman at her back, boot slipping across the cave floor.

Her escape instantly cut off by the killer. "You're not going anywhere." A flashlight beam launched directly for her, but it was Patrick's fist that slammed into her chest.

The impact crushed precious oxygen from her lungs,

and she collapsed back into Mae's arms. Sputtering coughs were all she could manage. She kicked against the floor to straighten her torso, to make it possible to breathe, but it was as though she'd gone into spasm. Her body didn't know what to do, how to get that next breath. Sayles grabbed for her throat, heart rate so high in the rafters she feared it would never come down.

Mae's sobs filled her ears.

And she was finally able to take a breath.

Elias's strike to the killer's throat turned the bastard's attention off her. The brutality of his attacks—precise and controlled in perfect sync—told of experience far beyond anything she'd ever seen. And gave her a glimpse of the violence that could've turned on her at any point during her marriage.

She scrambled onto all fours, still out of breath but able to move. "We have to get out of here. We have to go. Now."

"How?" Mae interlaced her hand with Sayles's. Desperation filtered in through the tight grip capable of blocking blood flow to her fingers. "They're blocking our escape."

She was right. And despite Elias's combat expertise, the Hitchhiker Killer was holding his own. Taking and delivering blows that would surely wear Elias down within minutes. He'd survived a fall from 1,000 feet. There was no telling what internal injuries he'd already sustained or if the next hit would kill him. She couldn't leave him here, but she couldn't ask Mae to stay. Her ex-husband had come for her, killed six people to find her and wouldn't hesitate to make her the seventh if she ran again. He'd never stop coming for her. Never stop hunting her.

"Run!" Elias struck with his left fist, then the right, grabbing the killer's wrist. He yanked the joint hard enough the cave filled with a pop and quickly launched his opposite hand into his opponent's chest.

The Hitchhiker Killer stumbled back. Rubbed at his chest as though he'd merely been inconvenienced. "No, Sayles. Stay. You know what happens if you run. What I'll do to you once I've finished off Agent Broyles. What I'll do to my darling Mae."

A whimper from behind chilled the blood in Sayles's veins. This. This was what she'd been afraid of all these months. Knowing her ex was still out there, wanting to hurt her, to make her pay for having the courage to leave. She'd broken his rules, after all, thought of herself for once and summoned the will to leave, and the possibility of him finding her had kept her in a permanent state of paranoia since. Numbness that'd taken months to shed infiltrated her nervous system and held her paralyzed. One breath. Two. Any minute now she'd lose all control, and there would be nothing she could do.

"Sayles!" Elias's demand barely reached through the white noise of blood rushing into her ears. The flashlight in his hand flickered as if traumatized by the violence, like the new light inside her chest. A light that a cocky, relentless, merciless federal agent had lit over the past two days. "Sayles, you can do this! Fight!"

Fight. Hadn't that been what she'd been doing for so long? Fighting to cope with the viciousness of a man who'd sworn to love her until death. Fighting for her life after her arrest for a murder she hadn't committed. Fighting to make it one day to the next while behind bars when it felt like the entire world had turned against her. Fighting. She was so…tired of fighting.

But that didn't make the war disappear.

And for the first time since she'd come to Zion, she wasn't alone. Clarity sharpened as Elias clutched the flashlight and shot his fist into the killer's face. He'd been rooting for her the moment they'd been thrust together on this assignment. Empowering her to trust herself, to break free of the self-inflicted weight she insisted on carrying these past few months. Showing her what real power looked like.

And she could do the same for other womn who'd been in her position.

Mae had been living through hell. So thoroughly tortured without the man ever needing to lay a hand on her. But she and Mae could rewrite the narrative. They could take that first step together. Sayles strengthened her hold on the woman's hand and maneuvered Mae behind her, acting as a shield as Elias had done for her. "Stay behind me. No matter what happens, don't let go of my hand."

She felt more than saw Mae's agreement.

Her partner took the opportunity to lunge. He threw what looked like everything he had into rocketing his fist into the killer's face but missed. Bringing his elbow up, he blocked the next assault, but the one after landed its mark. Elias stumbled back into the wall, unable to get his balance as the Hitchhiker Killer attacked.

Now, Sayles kept to the wall, dragging Mae behind her. The killer's flashlight rolled closer as he and Elias battled for dominance with gut-wrenching violence, but the Hitchhiker Killer's attention remained solely on survival. On winning. That was the kind of man he was. The kind that needed to control, to dominate and come out on top, but Sayles wouldn't give up little pieces of herself to avoid the consequences of that rage anymore. She'd face them head-on and help Mae do the same by getting them out of this cave.

The killer pinned Elias against the far wall, both hands around his neck. Her partner rained hits down on to the bastard's forearms, but the Hitchhiker Killer refused to loosen his grip. Elias's face seemed to swell in the dim light of the flashlight rocking back and forth across the rock floor from the commotion. Pinched in a way that told her he wasn't getting any oxygen. He was dying right in front of her, forcing her to choose between saving Mae or saving him.

There wasn't a choice. There never had been when it came to Elias.

Sayles grabbed for the flashlight and shoved it into Mae's hand. "Go. Get out of here. Run east as fast as you can. Don't stop. There's a trail there that will take you down in the Narrows. Find somewhere to hide, out of sight. National park rangers will find you in the morning."

"What about you?" Terror etched into Mae's face. The thought of being alone—of dying alone—clearly scared her and she gripped onto Sayles's forearm.

"Get to the Narrows. You can do this. I promise. Go." Maneuvering Mae ahead of her, she nodded. "It's all going to be okay."

It was a promise she'd needed to hear in the middle of the storm. She couldn't force Mae to believe her, but someday she could look back and see the rainbow peeking through the clouds.

The woman didn't have to be told twice, her outline blending in with shadow and darkness as she ran for the cave's entrance. Hiking through the backcountry without supplies brought its own set of complications. In the dark held more dangers, but Mae was strong. She just didn't know it yet.

Strength drained from Elias's attempts to get free. The weak beam coming off his discarded flashlight revealed he'd lost enough consciousness his eyes had fallen closed. She was already moving. Jumping. She secured her arms around the killer's neck and pulled as hard as she could to break his grip on Elias. They fell as one. Then came the pain. Her head snapped back against the unforgiving cave floor. Another round of bright lights exploded behind her eyes. Weight vanished from her front.

"You just don't know when to give up, do you, Ranger Green?" The Hitchhiker Killer stood above her. How he'd moved so quickly when she was still reeling from the impact, she had no idea. "I guess now is as good a time as any to punish you for coming between me and my wife."

Coughing punctured through the high-pitched ringing in her ears. Elias. Was he hurt? She couldn't afford to take her eyes off the man in front of her.

"That's one decision I will never regret." Sayles scrambled to her feet, unsteady but determined to buy Mae as much time as possible. She was out of her depth, facing off with a man who'd killed multiple people, some full-grown men, but she wouldn't budge. Not because of him. "And she's not your wife. Men like you believe you're owed everything you set your sights on. I'm proof that we're strong enough to fight back."

She didn't give him the chance to respond, throwing her fist directly at his face.

He stepped out of her path, and her momentum carried her forward. Too far. Too close. Sayles braced for the attack, but it never came. Adjusting to put him front and center and block his path to the cave's entrance, she swung again. And missed. That crazed smile that didn't quite show his teeth and deepened the cracks around his eyes triggered a chill in her bones. He was toying with her. Making her believe she had a chance only to pull the rug out from underneath her when he got too impatient. A mouse trapped beneath a cat's paw.

"I must say, Ranger Green, I'm quite disappointed. Surely, NPS trained you better than to provoke a predator." The Hitchhiker Killer hauled his foot into her chest.

She was flying, her legs swinging out from under her. Slamming into the cold floor. Sayles rolled onto her side. Pain radiated from her shoulder to her hip and across her torso as she sucked in a shallow breath. It was all she could manage.

The second kick emptied her lungs and cracked something vital.

Her scream drilled through her head. The barest hint of moonlight filtered through the darkness ahead. The entrance. Escape. To lead the killer away from Elias. To put herself between him and Mae. She owed it to them both. Every cell in her body screamed for her to move, but all she could do was push off with her toes. Gaining nothing but a few inches of distance at a time. She felt more than saw the killer's presence at her back. Watching her suffer, enjoying the power it gave him.

"You can't protect her. No matter where she runs, I'll find her. I wasn't lying about the tracker in her mouth. Though now I suppose she'll try to have it removed." Weight stacked on top of her calf, halting her in place. "In the end, she'll still belong to me, and I will kill any man who dares put his hands on what's mine before I take it out on her."

Sayles had heard it all before—lived it. He wasn't anything special, but someone somewhere had taught him he didn't have to work for the things he wanted. Taught him he was owed. "Are you finished with your villain speech? I was promised turkey when this case was over, and I've got to tell you, I'm starving."

The third kick hiked her off the floor and upturned her entire world. Gravity shifted from the center of her body to the edges as the ground ripped out from underneath her. Needles of pain clawed across the exposed skin of her face and arms. She was in free fall, out of control and moving too fast to stop down the mountain face. Three times. Four. Her spine curved around a boulder, a cry spilling into the night.

The killer's outline crossed the path of moonlight staring down on her. This park had saved her life. She should've known it would require something in return. Sayles struggled to breathe around the jagged pain in her rib cage. "It's over, Ranger Green. Look at you. You can't save anyone. You can't even save yourself."

But she had. With Elias's help.

A second outline cleared through the shimmer of disorientation. Or was she seeing double? Movement slashed over the Hitchhiker Killer's shoulder. He jerked in place. Then dropped to his knees and onto his face. Elias tossed a rock at his feet, kneeling beside her to scoop her against his chest. "That guy talks too much."

Chapter Twenty-Eight

"Ow." The park medic prodded at the contusion bubbling from Elias's forehead with a little too much force. He tried to jerk back but didn't get far. The back of his head hit the ambulance door and triggered a whole new headache.

"Hold still or I'll sedate you, Agent Broyles." Okay. There was a witch underneath the expertly done makeup, platinum-blond hair and gum snapping. Ranger Barbie was actually a sadist. His investigative skills had failed him.

The first morning rays of a new day made him sick to his stomach. Then again, that could be the fact that he hadn't eaten anything substantial in three days, fought a killer determined to gut him and fallen from 1,000 feet off the side of a cliff. But what did he know? He narrowed his gaze on the ranger setting a butterfly bandage across his forehead. Honestly, he hadn't even known he'd hit his head while fighting the Hitchhiker Killer. At least, not until Sayles had winced looking at his face. "You're not as nice as you look."

"I get that a lot." Another snap of her gum. She set piercing blue eyes made for magazine covers on him with a slow spread of her lips. Demonic. That was the word that came to mind. "Comes in handy for one-night stands. They can't leave fast enough."

Shock caught in his throat. Elias had to swallow to keep himself from spitting all over her pressed uniform with laughter. "I'll warn whoever I can." At the moment, that included Grant, who'd interrupted Elias's physical exam twice now to ask Ranger Barbie about a mole on his back. Then his front.

Elias closed his eyes and set his head back against the ambulance bay door. He and Sayles had somehow dragged themselves back to Mae and Javier's tent after their face-off with the killer. The radio hidden inside had given them direct contact with Risner and search-and-rescue. Since the helicopter couldn't retrieve them at night, they'd had to settle in beside a dead man and wait until the sun crested the horizon in the east. Another team had been sent up the Narrows to retrieve Mae, who was currently wrapped in a solar blanket on one of the park benches with an oxygen mask strapped over her face. Alive. Traumatized, but alive. She and Javier had been on their honeymoon. Married just two months ago, they'd chosen to take a road trip across the country to start their new life off with adventure. Right around the time bodies had started turning up on the interstate.

The Hitchhiker Killer, identified as Patrick Corrl— yes, he'd actually given Sayles his real name—had been airlifted in a basket. And right into a body bag. Now that the case was concluded, each of the victims would be returned to their families for burial or cremation, including Javier and the hiker murdered at the base of the Narrows.

"You're good to go. Keep it clean and dry, and there will be minimal scarring." Ranger Barbie shucked the bright pink latex gloves she'd donned to examine and treat his injuries and tossed them into the biohazardous waste bin in the rig. "You know, I think my mom said the same thing about the first time I had sex. She wasn't wrong."

"Thank you for that visual, Ranger Jordan." Elias shoved to stand. Mistake. He'd made a mistake. His bones hurt. Was that possible? Hell, how they'd managed to escape with nothing more than a few bruises and cuts—well, apart from his broken nose and Sayles's cracked ribs—he didn't know. Some X-rays were in order.

"I can go all night." Was every word out of Ranger Barbie's mouth meant to be sexual?

Elias wasn't interested in finding out and left her to pack her supplies. There was only one woman on his mind. Searching the parking lot, he headed for the visitors' center. Away from the chaos of Risner giving the media snippets of the harrowing assignment his department had taken on, Grant's incessant attempt to get Ranger Barbie's attention and law enforcement rangers begging to confirm his statement for the fourth time. The tug he'd experienced while racing to find Sayles led him through the visitors' center's tinted glass doors and toward the theater seating set up for hikers heading out of the trails.

The exact location he'd first set eyes on her.

That intense green gaze snapped to him as he approached. He couldn't shut down the flinch as he took in the bruising across her face and a matching butterfly bandage on her chin. Taking a seat next to her on the bench, Elias fought against the pain in his torso. New dressings pulled at the skin across his side and along his inner thigh, but he'd yet to change into a fresh set of clothes. "To think just a few days ago you were trying to get out of this assignment. Look how far we've come."

"I'm still debating if I made the right choice." Sayles

set her head against his shoulder, and the ricocheting pain vanished with her warmth. They stared at the dark theater screen, almost closed off from the rest of the world in this small corner of the building. "You owe me a turkey."

He couldn't contain his laugh. "I remember." And he had every intention of following through.

"How is she?" Sayles didn't have to specify who she meant. He could see Mae through the front doors from their position.

"Alive thanks to you." Angling his nose against her scalp, he kissed the top of her head. Not daring to pull away. Not wanting to be apart from her for a second longer. Neither of them had slept during the night—too keyed up, too desperate to prove they'd survived. He'd held her, but his brain still wasn't convinced this wasn't just some part of a nightmare he couldn't wake up from. "No one else with your past would've done what you did, putting yourself between her and her abuser. You saved her life."

"Did I?" The words were almost too soft for him to pick up, and if he hadn't been totally and completely tuned into every minor shift in this woman, he might've missed it. "Because from where I'm sitting, she's leaving this place a lot more traumatized than when she arrived. Not only did her ex try to kill her. but her new husband is dead. Shot right in front of her."

"You saved her life, Sayles. You gave her the gift of slaying her demons and moving on, of never having to look over her shoulder again." Securing his arm around her back, he hauled her against him. Putting them flush against each other shoulder to hip. Right where she belonged. "How many women in her position can say that? You made that happen. She owes you her life."

"She doesn't owe me anything. She's free. That's all I ever wanted for her. And for me." She straightened, notching her chin higher to look him dead in the eye. "And I got it. Thanks to you."

He didn't understand. "What do you mean?"

"These past few days, I was so determined to hate you. Not you specifically, but what you represented. I'd convinced myself all federal agents had to be like my ex-husband because why else wouldn't have anyone seen what was going on in my marriage? Why wouldn't they have said something unless there was this unspoken code to always have another agent's back?" Shrugging, she relaxed into him further. "I made you the enemy, and I'm sorry. When you asked what our future held, I got scared. I was afraid if I gave you a chance to show me that you weren't anything like him, I would be handing over my freedom to live life how I wanted all over again. I never meant for you to feel you weren't enough like I was made to feel, and I hate that your heart was the casualty. But more, I hated the fact that I didn't hate you. In a way, I was holding myself prisoner. You showed me how to free myself."

His heart shuddered in his very sore chest. "Does that mean you like me?"

"I'm saving my conclusions until after our first date." Slipping her palm against his chest, she smacked him lightly. That breathtaking smile lit up her whole face. "No, Agent Broyles, it means I'm falling for you. Of course, I didn't realize it until you went over the side of a cliff, and by then it was too late to tell you."

"Good thing I'm a lot harder to kill than I look." Elias tilted her head back with an index finger under her chin and pressed his mouth to hers. He kissed her until his mouth was swollen and his body tingled. Until every second of fear and desperation leaked from his nervous system and dissipated between them. "Will it make you feel better for almost letting me die without knowing how you felt if I tell you I'm falling for you, too?"

"Maybe." She traced a finger along his jaw, prickling the scruff on his face. Three days without shaving or a shower, but she didn't seem to mind. "But will you be taking those feelings back with you to Las Vegas now that the case is closed?"

Silence settled between them. Just for a moment as he considered the risk in admitting this thing between them had somehow grown to overshadow anything else in his life. "After I told you about my dad's death, you said it sounded as though I'd accepted my fate and that there was nothing I could do to change it. You weren't wrong. I've spent so long trying to live up to his legacy, to prove I could be good enough to catch the people who killed him, that it gradually became everything I am, and I let it. But I don't want that anymore."

Sayles pulled away. Not out of reach—because he wasn't sure either of them could handle that after everything they'd been through—but to get a better look at him. "What are you saying?"

"I'm saying..." He took a deep breath. Took the leap. "I'm saying I don't want my career to be all I am anymore. I want more out of life, and I want you in it. As much as possible. If that means quitting the FBI and signing on with Springdale's police department, I will. Because you're worth it."

Her mouth parted on a soft exhale. "Okay."

"Okay?" His laugh vibrated through him, and he

rocked back in his seat, taking her with him. "I spill my guts, almost literally after losing that fight with a damn twig, and all you have to say is okay?"

"Am I supposed to put up more of a fight?" She smoothed her fingers along the collar of his T-shirt with an answering smile of her own. "The truth is, I was thinking of making some changes, too."

Damn, he couldn't get enough of this woman. Would never let her go. "What kind of changes?"

"The moving on kind." She traced the length of his throat with one finger, and her smile slipped. "I can't forget what my ex did to me, but I think it's time to stop living in the past. To start making choices full of joy instead of fear. On my terms rather than out of a sense of survival."

Elias couldn't stop staring at this magnificent creature who'd been thrown in his path a mere three days ago. "Am I one of those choices?"

"That depends." Her smile was back in place, spreading slowly and revealing a playfulness he'd only glimpsed during their times in the Narrows. And, hell, he couldn't be more grateful she trusted him with the real her.

She had him hook, line and sinker. Or rather flash floods, death-defying falls and one-person tents. "On what?"

Her stomach growled, and Sayles kissed the corner of his mouth. "On how fast you can get me that turkey you promised."

* * * * *